DAGGER OF THE MIND

by

BOB SHAW

LONDON
VICTOR GOLLANCZ LTD
1979

© Bob Shaw 1979

ISBN 0 575 02612 X

Printed in Great Britain by Bristol Typesetting Co. Ltd,
Barton Manor, St Philips, Bristol

PART ONE

Petit mal

CHAPTER 1

IT WAS WHILE he was pouring his breakfast coffee that Redpath became aware that something was wrong.

He paused for a moment and looked around the small apartment, straining his ears for an extra sound or a missing sound in the murmurous background noise of the building. The apartment block was coming to life in exactly the same hesitant but inevitable manner which was familiar to him from a thousand other mornings, with nothing out of kilter anywhere. He could *feel* the young couple directly above moving about in an ambience of hurried sex, drip-dry garments hanging like ghosts in the gallows of the doorways, moraines of toast crumbs and marmalade on the butter, and on the sideboard the holy trinity assembled into a neat pile—cigarettes, money and car keys. He could feel old Mr Coates next door slowly regaining consciousness, simultaneously relieved and disappointed over not having died in the quiet hours of the night. On the other side, Harv Middleton, sales representative handling plug-in plastic lettering for menus in café windows, but who liked to tell people he was "in advertising", had already departed for the day in a cloud of conflicting perfumes. Everything was normal in the rest of the building, so the trouble had to be nearer at hand, within the four walls of Redpath's own apartment.

He took stock of the kitchen, noting the presence and position of every object, remembering stories of how people who have been burgled sometimes fail to miss a familiar item until months afterward. Again, there was no identifiable cause for his unease, which suggested that it did not have an external source—that the subtle wrongness was developing behind his eyes, between his ears, inside his skull. He tried testing himself. Those rays of sunlight slanting down on to the parquet-patterned floor covering—were they too yellow, too bright, too cheerful? That stencilled blue-and-bronze design on his coffee mug—had it acquired new merits, was it evoking too much aesthetic pleasure? Were there exotic fragrances, such as those of Chamberyzette or champak blossoms, mingling with the ordinary homely smells of his food and drink? In short—was he experiencing an aura?

No, please, no, Redpath thought. *Not today.*

He went to the long chromium-rimmed mirror in the bedroom and stood close to it. The image which looked back at him in spurious intimacy was that of a tall, slim-built man in his early thirties, with closely waved auburn hair and fair, dry, freckled skin of the type which seems never to perspire. There was an irresolute, mobile quality about the mouth which could make its owner look humorous, reckless or sullen on the instant, and the brown eyes were direct and inquisitive. The overall picture was one of unobtrusive good health, something for which Redpath usually felt grateful in view of the fact that he suffered from an incurable disease. There were other times, however, when—even if only for the assistance it would afford him in the management of his condition—he felt it would be more appropriate and in some way satisfying if he could appear ill.

In the present instance, as a case in point, he had no way of knowing if he was experiencing the aura which preceded a *grand mal*, actually undergoing a mild psychomotor epilepsy with its characteristic disturbance of thought, or simply passing through a period of heightened awareness which had no connection with neural abnormality. He decided to take precautionary measures.

Setting his coffee aside, he went into the living-room, picked up a cigar-box full of darts and positioned himself before the dartboard hanging near the window. With his toes at the edge of a carpet tile he knew to be exactly nine feet from the board, Redpath began throwing the darts, concentrating to the utmost as he tried to place one in each division from one to twenty. There were twenty-one darts in the box, which allowed him to make only one mistake in the private contest. He had to make two attempts at the four, a shot he usually found difficult, but that had the effect of steadying his hand and eye, and he success-fully picked off all the other numbers. In a second game he

8

needed two darts for both the four and the sixteen, but in the third set he went right round the board without a single miss, leaving himself with a dart in hand. He resisted an impulse to throw the remaining dart at the bull's eye—aware that hitting it could cause a dangerous surge of elation—and again took inventory of all those intangibles which made up his consciousness.

He felt cool, relaxed, fully locked-on to his surroundings.

Dr Hyall had recommended occupational therapy as a preventative for attacks—(*"It's a long-established fact that a workman rarely has a seizure while he's at the bench."*)—and for a time Redpath had tried making jewellery and repairing watches, but all crafts had a disadvantage in that it took too long to become engrossed, to pick up yesterday's threads. The darts, by comparison, provided him with immediate and complete involvement for hand, eye and mind. In spite of some scepticism from Dr Hyall and others, Redpath was satisfied that they shunted excesses of neural energy into harmless channels.

He retrieved his coffee and carried it back into the kitchen, now feeling a slight sense of anti-climax. *You can't win*, he thought. *And it's all Leila's fault—she should have been here this morning.*

Redpath finished his coffee, placed the mug in the sink beside his empty cereal dish and ran some hot water on both. That done, and with fifteen minutes in hand before he had to leave for the institute, he felt sufficiently bolstered to face the morning paper and mail which had been lying on the hall floor since he got up. He went into the hall and knelt to retrieve the various items spilled across the doormat. On top was a buff envelope bearing the return address of Harrup & Phizackeley, Estate Agents, and he knew it was yet another reminder about the rent of the apartment, now three months in arrears. He fingered the envelope, noted that it seemed to contain more than one sheet of paper, and wondered if things had gone beyond the reminder stage. That, he decided, was a mystery whose unveiling could wait until the evening. He flicked the unopened envelope onto the hallstand and glanced at the three other letters, identifying them as two promotional circulars and an electricity bill. What was the small ad he used to see in American pulp magazines? "DO YOU GET INTERESTING MAIL?"

He sighed and, still kneeling on the floor, turned his attention to the newspaper which was the *Haverside Herald*, a daily serving the four towns and scattering of hamlets which made up the South Haverside district. He took it in preference to any of the nationals because, although the *Herald* did its best to be as despondent as any major paper, the tragedies served up in its pages were usually on a manageable scale and allowed Redpath to go on believing that something could be done. One of the front page stories in that day's edition was a case in point—it concerned a local pigeon fancier who had just lost a third batch of prize racing birds.

"It is definitely sabotage of some kind," said 54-year-old Mr Giddings at his home last night. "My birds made good time the whole way from France, and they were definitely seen passing over the Tiverly Edge checkpoint at ten o'clock on Sunday morning, which means they should have been——"

Redpath stopped reading as he became aware of something peculiar. At this time of the day the corridor outside his apartment received a lot of natural light, creating a thin line of silver radiance along the bottom of Redpath's door. The strip of brightness was there now, but it was interrupted at the centre—which meant that an object had been placed against the outside of the door, or that somebody was standing there. The former explanation was the most likely—the postman sometimes simply abandoned packages that were too big for the letterbox—but it seemed to Redpath that the ends of the dark segment were wavering slightly, as became the shadow of a living thing. On the other hand, there was no sound, no evidence that a caller was getting ready to ring the doorbell, and it was hard to believe that anybody would be eccentric enough to stand vigil on his threshold. It had to be a package. The slight shimmering had to be a trick of the light, a result of foliage stirring in the tall trees behind the building or of clouds slipping across the disc of the sun.

Redpath stood up and reached for the lock, then *something* happened inside his head. There was a shifting, a disturbance, a psychological event. He found himself looking at the plastic-rimmed lens of the peephole set in the middle of the door, the absurd device he had never used because it was designed for nervous and neurotic old ladies. He brought his eye close to the lens.

The face on the other side was not immediately recognisable as a face. At first there was an impression of mushy redness, as though he was looking at a giant tomato or some crimson-fleshed fruit from which the skin had been removed, leaving a surface of moistly-oozing pulp. There was a moment during which human features began to emerge from the glistening mass, followed by a brief period of rejection in which Redpath's mind refused to deal with the messages it was receiving. Then came the instant of terrible, gut-churning, soul-blighting acceptance.

The face, the entire head, had been stripped of skin, creating what appeared to be a nightmarish sculpture in gelled blood. The eyes and eyelids, which were complete in every detail except for lashes, were complex spheres of blood; the naked flesh of the lips was parted to reveal blood-enamelled teeth; the nose, made pendulous by the distortions of the peephole lens, glittered as a mass of bloody droplets, and dark-red bubbles welled and swelled beneath the nostrils, showing that the monster was alive . . .

Redpath moaned aloud as he stepped back from the door, then a survival mechanism came into play, forcing him against his will to do what had to be done. He lurched forward, twisted the handle of the Yale lock and pulled the door wide open.

The corridor was empty.

He advanced into it on rubbery legs and looked about him. To his left the corridor came to a dead end a short distance on the far side of the door of Mr Coates' apartment. On the right was Harv Middleton's door, beyond it the head of the stairs which led down to street level, and in the opposite wing of the building three more doors, all locked. Through the windows which ran the length of the corridor he could see mature plane trees, part of a cindery car park, a builder's yard stacked with concrete lamp standards, and the rear elevations of a row of semi-detached houses and assorted garages. Morning sunlight glowed on everything with quiet intensity. The world looked cheerful, humdrum, commonplace.

Everything's normal except me, Redpath thought. *I'm turning into a frigging maniac.*

He went back into his living-room and stood drumming with his fingertips on the arm of a chair while he came to an important decision about the course of his life. His work—his so-called work—at the institute represented his sole source of income, but he was not going to carry on with it if this was the sort of thing he could expect. The pay was pretty poor anyway—not enough to live on, but just sufficient to convince the social security people, who put commercials on TV begging the public to come and accept money from them, that he was a malingering spendthrift. If he had no work at all he would qualify for National Assistance, would get his rent arrears taken care of, and—above all—would be able to resume a life that was as normal as anybody with his particular affliction could hope to achieve.

Find a cheaper place, came a stray thought. *A safer place.*

What could be safer than this place?

Safe from what?

"I told you," Redpath said indignantly to the peacefully inert furniture. "I'm turning into a lollipop farmer." He lifted his brown suede zipper-up, pulled it on and strode out of the apartment, slamming the door behind him. The corridor was still empty. When he got down to street level flat swirls of dust and candy wrappers blew in from the footpath to greet him, gambolling around his ankles like pets. Redpath stared down at them in distaste, suddenly realising how much he had come to detest the place where he lived.

Bingham Terrace was named after a prominent councillor in Calbridge, largest of Haverside's four towns. The novelty of the location had appealed to Redpath at first. It had seemed like a fun idea to live on a high street, right in the heart of things, watching the world go by from the vantage point of his cosy apartment perched above a row of six shops. For quite a long time he had appreciated the nearness and convenience of the shops, and had gone to considerable lengths to get on friendly terms with their owners and staffs. Their assorted specialties—home bakery, newsagent, boutique, coffee shop, grocer, butcher—might, for the most part, have been chosen to suit his personal needs. Even the one exception, the women's clothiers, had managed to make a contribution because its sign proclaimed it to be *The Boutique Shop*. After Redpath had pointed out the tautology to the girls who worked there, he had established himself as a comic by putting his head round the door once a week and saying he wanted to buy a shop.

Now, quite abruptly, he was tired of the raw modernity of the place, the noise of the passing traffic and the eternal slamming of car doors, the racket kicked up by the youngsters who hung around the coffee shop in the evenings. None of the people in the other eleven apartments had fully responded to his overtures of friendship—possibly because the word had gone round that he was an epileptic and they were slightly afraid of him, more possibly because they were dull and circumscribed beings leading dull and circumscribed lives. In all probability he had never managed to get through to them, not even once.

Standing in the narrow passageway which constituted the entrance to the upstairs apartments, Redpath frowned into the boutique on his right, intensifying his gloomy mood. Two of the girls had already arrived, but were standing with their backs to him, arranging displays on a counter, thus making it impossible for an exchange of friendly signals.

They probably never got the joke anyway, he thought. *Communication problems. They probably laugh out of politeness. Or nervousness. I should have spelled it out that first time. Look, boutique is French for shop, so your sign says that this is a shop shop. Get it? See the funny joke?*

Redpath found himself wishing, more fervently than before, that Leila Mostyn had spent the night with him. He was convinced that everything would have been all right had she been there beside him when he had wakened an hour previously. And no less an authority than Doctor Hyall agreed that he would benefit from the comfort and support of a stable relationship. He squared his shoulders and walked through the tunnel-like passageway to the car park at the rear of the building. Barred by law from obtaining a driving licence, he had the distinction of being the only person in Bingham Terrace—old Mr Coates included—who did not have a car, and his pedal cycle was the sole occupant of a lean-to in one corner of the cindered rectangle. Still brooding about Leila, he unchained the bicycle and wheeled

13

it out to the street. The girls in the boutique saw him this time and waved a greeting. Redpath halted and pointed up at the sign above the shop, and the girls shook with extravagant laughter.

"Who's kidding who around here?" Redpath muttered, getting on to the bicycle. He rode with the townward traffic for a couple of hundred yards before turning left into a quieter and mainly residential thoroughfare which would take him most of the way to the Jeavons Institute. The purr of his tyres on the tarmac and the steady rhythm of his legs usually served as aids to thought. He tried to rehearse the resignation speech he was going to make to Henry Nevison, but his mind kept turning towards that other source of the complications which had begun to plague his life.

Leila Mostyn was a mathematician who for six months had been doing post-graduate work on statistics in the research department where Redpath passed most of the working day. On meeting Redpath, and learning what he did for a living, she had spent some weeks treating him with impersonal kindliness, like a cancer researcher being very correct in her handling of a laboratory animal she would soon have to dissect. For his part, Redpath had been captivated by her white-coated, tweed-skirted, straight-backed, pale-lipped air of sexual abstemiousness.

He had set out to court her, using all his resources of imagination and intellect, and for a full month after they had begun spending occasional nights together he had gone around in a romantic daze. Self-consciousness about his health and poor financial prospects had kept him from proposing marriage, but he had hoped they might gradually be drawn into a formal commitment as the sensual side of Leila's character continued to develop. That had been a good month. Then had come the discovery that she was not austere by nature—merely discreet and independent. The reason she would spend only one night a week with him on average was that she often preferred to be alone, and in between times felt free to choose any partner from a circle of male friends at whose extent Redpath could only guess.

He had been hurt and angry, the more so because he knew he had been tricked by his own naïve egocentricity. Since then he had come to accept the situation, and even to see advantages in

14

it at times, but his attitude was a precarious one. He was well aware that any attempt to monopolise Leila would mean the end of the relationship and yet at least once a day he got a suicidal urge to express his jealousy, to remonstrate with her for not feeling as he did, to start laying down rules for another person's behaviour. The urges grew stronger each time there was a setback in his daily routine—the implication being that she had carelessly denied him earthly paradise—and he had even reached the stage of holding her responsible for variations in his state of well-being. He knew this was illogical and childish, but he was unable to prevent himself from doing it.

It's all too much, he thought. *I've got to find a safer place.*

The psychophysiology department of the Jeavons Institute was housed separately in a brown sandstone edifice, built in the middle of the 19th century, which looked as though it had originally been the home of a wealthy merchant. It was screened from the granite façade and stainless steel cloisters of the institute proper by a row of Scots pines and some very old rhododendrons which had assumed the height and volume of modest-sized dwellings. Even on a fine summer day it was dank and cool as an underground cave behind the barricades of foliage, and on the lawn there were many areas like permanent brown shadows where grass refused to grow. The gravel of the surrounding paths was always wet underneath, so that footprints and tyre tracks showed up as dark impressions which lingered for a long time, like infra-red images, until the surface stones dried out and lightened.

Redpath cycled on the deep gravel until its sliding shiftiness robbed him of all momentum, then dismounted and wheeled his machine to the department's front entrance. He propped it against the short stone balustrade at the side of the steps and went into the building. Leila Mostyn was coming out of her office as he entered the hall and she stopped to bid him good morning. She was a tall girl with cropped ash-blonde hair, grey eyes and a quirky fullness to her lips which to Redpath suggested every desirable feminine quality he could think of, from intelligence and humour to warmth and generosity. She was wearing what he thought of as the typical Leila Mostyn ensemble—a transparent blouse and a half-cup brassière of indisputably sexist design which would have put her figure on blatant display had she not added a countyish tweed skirt and a white lab coat. The coat in particular served as some kind of personal statement because nothing in her work made it necessary and nobody else in the department wore one.

Give a little, keep a lot. Let people know what they're missing. I wonder how she'd like it if, instead of meekly falling in with her every whim and piddling little plan, I walked into her flat and just took her any time I wanted, any way I wanted, whether she was in the mood or . . .

"John!" Leila gave him a quizzical smile. "What are you dreaming about?"

"Nothing." Redpath was startled by the savagery of the vision which had obscured his thoughts. He gave a guilty laugh.

"Did you get enough sleep last night?"

"Plenty," he said and, giving way to a jealous impulse, added, "How about you?"

The traces of Leila's smile vanished on the instant, showing there had been near-telepathic communication. "I slept very soundly, thank you."

This is pure madness, Redpath thought. *I'm committing suicide.* He grinned and said, "Shame, shame."

Leila drew the edges of her lab coat together at the front. "What do you mean?"

"The two of you lying there all night and nothing happening. It seems a bit of a waste."

Leila examined him coldly. "I think I'll suggest to Henry that he should give you a month off." She tried to walk away but Redpath caught her arm and was thrilled and taunted by the warmth of her flesh beneath the white cotton.

"Who was he, anyway?" he said, still grinning. "Anybody I know?"

"I've told you before, John—you really must try to get over your adolescent sexual hang-ups."

"That's what I'm doing. I asked you openly and frankly who you slept with last night, and if you haven't got any sexual hang-ups yourself you should give me an open and frank reply. Right?"

16

"Get lost, John."

"Rejection and hostility." Redpath released her arm and mimed writing something in a notebook. Leila turned quickly, launching circles of perfume into the air, and hurried away into the complex of partitioned rooms at the rear of the house, her sponge-soled flats making little hissing sounds on the tile floor. Redpath snorted in triumph. Leila was the one who usually used psychological jargon as a quiver of poisoned arrows and she had disliked it intensely when he had got in first. It meant, of course, that in less than a minute he had undermined months of patiently building or preserving a relationship, but he could sense that it was a time for big changes. He could feel it in the air. It was inevitable that his leaving the institute would drive a wedge between them, and it was better that he should take the initiative and break free of her while he still had his pride and dignity, rather than watch helplessly as she gradually rationed out less and less of her time to him, making him less and less of a man.

Pride? Dignity? Next thing it'll be white-sidewall tyres on the bike. Since when have you been lumbered with junk like pride and dignity?

Redpath shook his head, frowning, sprinted up the stairs and went along the first-floor landing to Nevison's office. He knocked lightly on the white-painted, panelled door and went in without waiting for a reply. Nevison, who was seated at his desk in the bay window, glanced up in surprise. He was a lean, professorial-looking man in his fifties, with bushy grey hair and a generally athletic appearance which was modified by a certain leaden colouring of his skin and a bluish-redness of the nostrils. His academic standing was very high, but he always made a point of addressing Redpath in ultra-clear, unadorned English. It was a practice for which Redpath had been grateful until he began to suspect that Nevison took pride in his ability to communicate with the common man and saw it as a useful scholarly adjunct.

"Hello, John," Nevison said. "You're early today. Please sit down."

"Thanks." Redpath lowered himself into a chair, as he did so realising for the first time that by unfailingly inviting him to take a seat Nevison had forestalled the development of a

17

situation in which Redpath would feel entitled to do so unasked. He considered rising and waiting until sitting down again could be seen as a unilateral action, then it occurred to him that such preoccupations were neurotic. Would he, Redpath wondered, have been like that a year ago? Was it all part of a pattern?

Nevison sat without speaking for a moment and then, as if he had been taking time to complete some important train of thought, brightened noticeably and said, "Well now, John—what can I do for you?"

"I want out of the project," Redpath said. He considered his words and decided he had not been sufficiently assertive. "In fact, I've made up my mind to quit."

Nevison looked concerned. "I get the impression that this is quite a sudden decision. Am I right?"

"Well . . ." Redpath was reluctant to answer, feeling he was giving something away. "What difference does that make?"

"Perhaps none. You are perfectly free to drop out at any time, you know that, but if there's some specific cause I'd like to discuss it with you and see what we can do about removing it. We don't want to lose you, John."

"Thanks, but I've made up my mind."

Nevison gave a wistful smile. "If we were in an industrial setting, this is the point where I would offer you more money, but I think you know the position with regard to our research grants. I live in dread of the day that word gets back to the South Haverside council that we're dabbling with telepathy. It's back to porridge for all of us when that happens."

"It isn't the money," Redpath said. "At least, that's only part of it."

"Oh." Nevison steepled his fingers and stared out through the high window. Sunlight reflected from the modern architecture of the main buildings created utopian glimmers in the palisade of dark green foliage.

Redpath felt impelled to speak. "I'm cracking up. It might be a build-up of the drugs, I don't know . . . I just know I'm not going on."

"Have you had a reaction?" Nevison said, leaning forward.

"Reaction!" Redpath huffed to express his sense of outrage. "This morning when I was picking up my mail I looked out

18

through the peephole in the door and I saw something straight out of a Hammer movie. There was this face, and it had been *skinned*. It was a face made out of raw beef. Running with blood. I don't have to put up with that sort of thing, Henry. Nobody can make me."

"It sounds rather unnerving," Nevison conceded, "but I'm sure there must be some quite prosaic explanation. Was the impression more vivid than those you've been getting in the routine tests?"

"It was totally convincing. It was just as if . . . Wait a minute! Are you saying I got a telepathic image?"

"What other explanation is there?"

"What *other* explanation? You haven't given me the first one yet." Redpath shifted restlessly in his chair, causing it to creak. "Are you trying to tell me that somewhere, somewhere near me, somebody was actually looking at a face like that? And that I picked up the mental image? It would be more comforting to believe I was going mad."

"There's no question of your going mad," Nevison said, assuming a didactic manner. "But just consider the circumstances and compare them with some of our test results. You had just got up, so your mind wasn't cluttered with day residue memories. If I remember the layout of your flat correctly the hall is fairly dark, so you had another trigger factor—a sudden drop in light intensity. And you looked through one of those spyhole devices, thus sharply limiting your field of view. Do you remember that quite early on we discovered what we call the small screen effect? It all adds up."

"The face," Redpath said quietly. "How about the face?"

"Yes, there's the problem of the face." Nevison stroked his chin for a moment. "We've also recorded one or two examples of inadvertent double transmission, haven't we? That row of shops you live above—is there a butcher there?"

"Yes, but his stock is very basic. There isn't much demand for flayed homo sapiens out our way."

"I'm suggesting—and this is just one possibility—that your local butcher may have been carving a flank of beef and thinking about somebody at the same time, and that this led to your picking up a dual transmission."

"That's wrong," Redpath said flatly. "That's all wrong."

"What's wrong with it?"

"It's a cooked-up thing."

"The specious is not necessarily untrue."

"I don't know about that, but . . ." Redpath paused as something flickered in his memory like the first tongue of flame that heralds an inferno. "You can forget about the small screen effect—what we're talking about started before I looked through the peephole. The only reason I looked through it in the first place is that when I knelt down to pick up my post I could tell by the light coming under the door that there was something outside.

"And I'll tell you another thing! Those spy lenses distort anything you see through them, and the face I saw was distorted . . ."

Nevison gave a smile whose kindliness was intended to show Redpath that he had said something exceptionally stupid. "So what you're implying is that this creature from a horror film was actually standing outside your door. In the flesh, as one might say, going by your description of it."

"I didn't imply that," Redpath said, wondering what he *had* implied.

"Of course not—I'm sorry. Having opened the hall door and found nothing unusual in the corridor, you must know better than anybody else that we're dealing with a subjective phenomenon. I mean, you did check outside, didn't you?"

"Yes."

"There you are, John. Proof."

Redpath nodded. "Proof I'm going mad."

"Forgive me for saying so, but your ideas of what constitutes madness appear to have been culled from Charlotte Brontë and Edgar Allan Poe—neither of whom was a psychiatric diagnostician of any standing." Nevison's lips twitched and Redpath knew he was pleased with his comment and was memorising it for later repetition.

"Call it what you like," Redpath said sullenly, becoming angry. "All I know is it was bloody frightening—the sort of thing I can well do without—and I blame it on the experiments."

"So do I," Nevison said unexpectedly, taking a new tack. "You must agree, John, that since we started treating you with

Compound 183 your telepathic ability, which was only vestigial in the beginning, has been enormously enhanced. Admittedly, we haven't yet developed a way to control the ability, but your radius of awareness is growing all the time, isn't it? You told me last week that when you wake up in the mornings you can sense what's going on in the other flats in your building. Correct?"

"I don't see what that's got to . . ."

"What I'm saying is that this is all new to us. It's beginning to appear that all mind-to-mind contacts don't take place on the conscious level—and all of us have monsters lurking around beneath the surface, John. Do you ever have nightmares?"

"Sometimes," Redpath said, feeling he was being manipulated.

"So do I. One has to accept them, and I imagine that with a little effort one could learn to live with the occasional daymare."

"One? That means me, doesn't it?"

"You're the focal point of the experiment, John." Nevison stood up, came round the desk and sat on the front edge of it close to Redpath, a manoeuvre which was intended to create an atmosphere of informal friendliness. "Look, I appreciate that you've had a disturbing experience, but it wouldn't be fair to any of us if you made a decision about your future while still in the aftermath. I'd like you to skip today's programme of tests and, instead, write or dictate a full report of what happened this morning, treating it as part of our experimental data. That shouldn't take very long, then you can have the rest of the day to yourself. Go for a walk and think things over, and we'll have another talk in the morning. How does that sound to you?"

"All right," Redpath said reluctantly, rising to his feet.

I'll hand in my resignation in writing. That'll make it official. No quibbling. All the soft soap in the world won't wash out a word of it.

He left Nevison without speaking further and went along the landing to the large room at the rear of the house which was used as an office by all those individuals who did not possess sufficient clout within the department to commandeer separate quarters. Of the six desks in the room only one was occupied that morning, by Terry Malan, a psychology student who was supposed to be working on a final year project, but who spent most of his time tinkering with motor cycle parts. He had a stripped-down

21

magneto spread out on his blotter and was staring at it with furrowed brow.

Redpath passed him in silence, sat down at his own desk and picked up a pen. He made up his mind to spend not more than ten minutes writing a brief report for Nevison and then to clear out for the rest of the day, but he quickly found that concentration was difficult.

Bubbles of blood swelling in the nostrils.

Is that the sort of thing one puts in a report? Is it attention to detail, or morbidity? Is it evidence of a scientific mind, or a sick one? How many men does Leila have? And how often? Where can I get another job? Why does that young creep Malan keep staring at me? I know he's staring at me, even though I can't see him. Every time he raises his eyes and looks at the back of my head it's like being caught in the beam from the Eddystone lighthouse. Should that go into the report, as well?

After an hour of sporadic scribbling Redpath had completed one page. He sealed it in an envelope, marked it "CONFIDENTIAL— FOR ATTENTION OF DR NEVISON," and placed it in the centre of his desk under a green slate paperweight. Aware he was acting as though he would not be returning, Redpath took a few personal possessions—postage stamps, emergency supply of phenobarbitone, nail clippers—from the desk's middle drawer and slipped them into his pocket. When he stood up to leave he found Malan watching him intently. Redpath winked at him, put his arms around an imaginary dancing partner and parodied a George Raft tango the whole way to the door, still without speaking.

Outside on the landing, he stood for a moment with a hand pressed to his forehead, suddenly afraid of himself. It occurred to him that it was madness to walk out on the experiment over a single incident which perhaps was never to recur—madness, not in the cackling-laughter-from-the-attic tradition Nevison had mentioned, but straightforward economic and social insanity. People were always making jokes about how easy it was to get money from the DHSS, but if his past experience was anything to go by they were likely to explain to him, very patiently, that if his surname began with R and he had the same number of fingers on each hand no benefit would be payable until after the next transit of Mercury. Then there was the prospect of cutting himself off from Leila, which was the last thing in the world he wanted to do.

He smoothed down his hair, brushed some flecks from the suede of his jacket and went down the stairs to find Leila. The hall floor stretched out before him, a subdued chessboard of pale green and biscuit-coloured tiles upon which moved blurred shadows of the outside foliage. All at once it was awash with blood.

This was not bright red, oxygenated blood such as he had seen on the apparition at the door of his apartment. It was *old* blood—brown, congealing, laced with black threads where it was smeared thin, filled with huge slug-like clots elsewhere. The clots glistened like mounds of raw beef. And, as if the underlying hall floor had been tilted, the hideous organic slime appeared to be flowing towards Redpath . . .

"*Ah, no,*" he whispered, gripping the banister with one hand and shielding his eyes with the other. He stood motionless for a moment, cringing, and when he uncovered his eyes the hall floor was clean again. Its leaf-embossed tiles might have been newly laid, newly worked over by the original Victorian housemaids with scrubbing brushes and carbolic acid and reeking wax polish. The rest of the world looked normal. A typewriter began a bored clacking in one of the offices nearby.

Redpath completed his descent of the stairs and walked thoughtfully into the rear of the building, urgent questions clamouring in his mind. They had told him that Compound 183 was a harmless derivative of enkephalin, modified to make it highly selective as to which brain cells it affected—but what did that mean? How long would its effects last? And what guarantee was there that Nevison, Magill and the others knew what they were talking about? After all, the very word "experiment" implied that they were only guessing, trying out different things, hoping that the guinea pig would not do something irritating like developing a tumour, or going mad, or dropping down dead.

The pay should have been higher. I've got to find a safer place.

He opened the door to Leila Mostyn's office and discovered she was not alone. Marge Rawlings, Nevison's secretary, was in a corner of the room using a photocopier which had been sited there for want of suitable space in other parts of the building. Judging by the stack of sheets at her side, she was going to be there for a long time.

"Good morning, ladies," Redpath called, hiding his disappointment. "And how are we today?"

"*We* are looking for somebody to help with this copying, and *you* are standing around with both arms the same length," Marge said, eyeing him hopefully through her gold-rimmed octagonal glasses. "How about it, John?"

"Sorry—I'm no good with machinery," Redpath said, turning his back to her and hunkering down beside Leila, who was seated at her desk and had her gaze fixed on a block of graph paper. She ignored his arrival.

"Leila," he whispered, touching her wrist, "I've got to talk to you."

She pulled her wrist away. "I'm busy."

"Look, I'm sorry about what I said."

"That makes no difference to my workload—I'm still busy."

He stared up at her face with helpless longing. "Can we have lunch together?"

Leila shook her head. "I'm going home to pick up some papers at lunchtime."

"Well . . ." Redpath shot a venomous glance over his shoulder at Marge Rawlings, who had stopped operating the photocopier and was maintaining an attentive silence. "I could go with you."

"Only if your bicycle goes as fast as my car," Leila said with casual cruelty.

"Leila!" He lowered his voice further. "Something's happening to me."

"Don't worry—it's called puberty."

"I see." Redpath tried unsuccessfully to think of a good riposte. "It's like that, is it?"

Leila picked up a pencil and began making dots on a graph sheet. Redpath waited a moment before accepting the dismissal, then straightened up and walked out of the office. Peals of laughter followed as soon as he closed the door. He stood in the green dimness, humiliated, aware that Leila was now discussing him with an office acquaintance, and his hands clenched into bony clubs. That laughter and bitch-talk—a desperate notion

24

came to him—could easily be silenced. Victory had been conceded to women in the war of the sexes, but being women they had not hampered themselves with anything as impractical as a victor's code of chivalry. How would it be if *he* broke the rules of fair play for a change? Women knew themselves to be the equals of men in those areas where they narrowly failed to be superior, but none of them was any good with fists. *Fists!* Redpath looked down at the complex, involuted weapons attached to the ends of his arms. There was a painful prickling on his forehead. The spiteful laughter and the bitch-talk would stop on the instant if he burst the office door open and went in and used his fists on Leila. One punch would carry her right out of the chair and spread her on the floor; another would wreck that supercilious, Tanqueray's-and-tonic, duvets and Bruckner's Fourth smile of hers; another would put fear in her eyes, and fear meant respect . . .

The front door of the house swung open and admitted a flood of light to the hall, light which penetrated into the narrower corridor-like section at the rear where Redpath was standing, making him feel he was under observation. He strode towards the door, brushed past the two men who had entered and plunged out into the mould-scented air.

A jetliner was climbing high in the sunlight, its con trail widening and breaking into curved white flakes. He grabbed his bicycle and wheeled it away against the drag of the gravel. As soon as he reached tarmac he got astride the machine, cycled out through the gates of the institute and turned in the direction of the town centre. The mid-morning lull had descended on the traffic and he was able to travel fast in top gear, the bicycle tilting from side to side as he put all his weight into each thrust on the pedals.

Redpath had almost reached the business section of Calbridge before it dawned on him that he had no idea where he was going. He braked abruptly, barely avoiding a collision with a mud-spattered grey Ford transit which had been behind him, and swung into the forecourt of a mock-Tudor pub. The outer doors of the pub were being latched open by a tubby man who nodded curtly to Redpath, surveyed the sky and retired inside to begin his day's work. Redpath got off the bicycle, sat down on the coping of the low brick wall surrounding the forecourt and tried to decide what to do next. The feeling was oddly similar to that which he had experienced on the one day he played truant from school—the places he was now free to go to no longer seemed worth the effort of getting there.

The classical refuge for a man in his position was the alehouse—and the shady interior of the pub beside him looked inviting—but a law he never broke was the one which decreed that alcohol and epilepsy did not mix. The alcohol itself could initiate an attack, the ingestion of large quantities of liquid was another potent trigger factor, and on top of all that there was the risk of a reaction from the anti-convulsant drugs in his system. He had learned to live with the constraints of his illness, telling himself that it was not being able to drink *or* drive which had kept him slim and fit, but on this particular morning it would have been good, very good, to be like other men. Everybody needed an escape door at some time or other, he concluded, rising to his feet, and it looked as though his would have to be an uplifting day of fresh air and solitude in the public park.

Ten minutes later he freewheeled into Calbridge's Churchill Gardens, a forty-acre rectangle of greenery which owed its existence to a liberal seeding of the area with World War II incendiaries. The schools had not yet begun the summer break so the park was quiet and almost empty. Redpath chained his cycle to a railing and walked towards the middle of the park, looking for a place in which to relax. He found a long seat overlooking a geometric display of flowers and sat down at one end of it, suddenly feeling tired and anticlimactic. Since breakfast time life had been beating him over the head in a steady rhythm, like two men sledging a single spike into the ground, and now that peace had descended he found it rather unnerving. It was too much like a prelude to even greater disasters.

Think, he told himself. *Draw up plans. This is the first day of the rest of your life.*

It was difficult, though, to project his thoughts into the future when the present and immediate past were filled with so much pain and confusion. The big question was—what had gone wrong? Everything that had happened that morning seemed to stem from the first attack of the horrors in his flat, but what had brought it on?

He had been out of work and without employment prospects when, two years earlier, he had volunteered to take part in a series of telepathy experiments at the Jeavons. His card-guessing scores had been the highest obtained from some eight hundred participants, and he had been elated when Henry Nevison had approached him subsequently and offered what seemed to be the greatest sinecure of all time. He was to be paid a monthly salary just to continue with the telepathy tests a few hours a day, five days a week, and his luck had really seemed to be in when—for once—it turned out that a prospective employer was undeterred by the fact of his having the falling sickness.

Redpath's mother had expressed alarm on hearing that the test programme included assessing the effects of a new family of psychotropic drugs on the telepathic facility, but he had managed to allay her fears. She was a naturally reticent woman, who had been turned into a near-recluse by irrational guilt over his condition, and it had come as a great relief to her to find that her son could earn money like a "normal" young man. Redpath was almost certain she had told her friends he was taking up medical research, but he had not objected. All his thoughts had been focused on his new occupation, his new mission in life.

In the early days he had been buoyed up by expectations of dramatic test results, but after some months that mood had faded and had been replaced by one of boredom. It was established beyond doubt that he did have a vestigial telepathic ability, but in such attenuated form that mathematicians usually had to be employed to differentiate between his performance and the workings of blind chance. Then had come Compound 183, and with it the gradual change not only in the statistics of his test results, but in the nature of his subjective experience. Instead of having to visualise a test card he had, on occasion, begun to *see* it. The ability was sporadic and uncontrollable to a large extent, but he had begun to feel that significant things were happening, that he, John Redpath, had been granted the privilege of, to use an overworked phrase of Nevison's, extending the boundaries of knowledge.

That had been the state of play when he had got out of bed less than three hours earlier, on what had promised to be a perfectly normal Tuesday morning . . .

27

Redpath's brooding was interrupted when a black-haired woman of about forty, who had been approaching at a leisurely pace, sat down on the seat beside him. He promptly experienced two distinct kinds of wonderment. The first was concerned with the way in which his mind, which had been preoccupied with dark terrors and the machinations of fate, immediately abandoned such exotic abstracts and turned to matters of Calbridge etiquette; and the second wonderment was on that homely, circumscribed level. He had been brought up in the South Haverside area and, although he had consciously shed his provincialism, its social conventions were second nature to him. In the protocol of the Four Towns, a woman who was alone in a park and wanted to rest would always choose an empty seat or bench, and if obliged to use a seat already occupied by a strange man would invariably position herself at the opposite end of it.

In this case, not only had the black-haired woman passed by a number of empty seats, she had sat down right beside Redpath, so close that their elbows were almost touching. And in Calbridge, even a prostitute—except for perhaps the most case-hardened—would be more circumspect than that. He glanced at the woman with some interest. Her face was swarthy and handsome, with heavy-lidded dark eyes and pouting, plum-coloured lips. It was the face, Redpath thought, of a gypsy queen—one whose people had known hard times, judging by her expression of rueful resignation. More than anything else, it was that expression which had led him to place her age at forty, for she had the ripe, full-busted body of a young woman who was just reaching the point at which she would have to start cutting down on her food. She was wearing a blue velvet jacket over a crimson T-shirt, faded Levis and dusty brown sandals.

"I'm dying for a smoke," she said casually. "Got a fag, love?"

Redpath, who had almost convinced himself of the woman's Romany origins, was surprised to hear the Nottinghamshire accent of his home town. "I'm sorry—I don't smoke."

She looked at him with raised eyebrows, smiling as though he had confessed to some shameful eccentricity she was prepared to forgive. "I'll just have to use my own then." She brought out a packet, extracted the last cigarette from it and flipped the packet into the centre of the path.

"That could cost you a hundred quid," Redpath said.

"It would be a good'un that got a hundred quid out of me, love." She lit the cigarette with a cheap Continental-style lighter and inhaled deeply.

Redpath noticed that her fingernails were grubby and that they had been lacquered in a nacreous brown which contrasted with the redness of her toenails. A trick of memory gave him an unexpected mental picture of a high school classmate of puritanical upbringing who had established a reputation as a rake by periodically declaiming, "I'm a great man for the slut." At the same time, and more unexpectedly, he experienced a powerful sexual attraction towards the woman, who appeared to be the opposite of Leila Mostyn in every way.

Hold on, John, he thought, alarmed. *You don't go in for all that crap about rebounds. You always said you were a human being, not a ping-pong ball. Remember?*

"What's wrong? you're not at work?" the woman said. "On your holidays?"

"No, I decided to have the day off."

"Just like that? It's well for some."

"I needed the break," Redpath said, wondering how long the oddly stilted conversation would go on.

The woman sighed. " I could do with a break. Seven days a week I work."

"Oh? What do you do?"

"I'm a landlady, would you believe." She gave a self-deprecatory laugh. "I run a boarding house."

"That's funny—I'm looking for a new place." The words had slipped out before Redpath had time to weigh the consequences. He stared down at his hands with an unaccountable feeling of nervousness.

"Is that a fact? I've got just the place for you. What's your name?"

"John." He resisted a weird juvenile impulse to give a false name. "John Redpath."

"I'm Betty York." The woman put her hand on his arm. "I've got just the place for you, John."

"I . . ." Redpath tried to force his brain into action. He had a firm conviction that Betty York's establishment would not be to his taste, but he had difficulty in finding a suitable way to turn down the proposal. "I was thinking of a self-contained flat."

"That's no use for you, love. All that expense and . . ." Her fingers squeezed his arm. ". . . no home comforts."

"I'm used to looking after myself."

"Ah, but it's not the same thing, is it?" She nudged him with her hip to make the message clear.

Redpath felt a guilty thrill. He needed a break, a holiday from the onerous task of being John Redpath; he also needed to revenge himself on Leila—and here, it seemed, was an opportunity to achieve both objectives at once. Everything with Leila, especially sex, had to be suffused with the white light of rationality, made aseptic, purged of any element which might give rise to archaisms such as obsessions, shame, anger, lust, jealousy, hatred, disgust, guilt—all those bitter leavenings which could turn the wine of love into a dark and dangerous brew, thus making it infinitely more satisfying. He could imagine the expression on her face if he let her know that he preferred being with a woman like Betty York, found pleasure in her coarseness and crude innuendos, her flaking nail polish and Lawrencian slum-dwellers' creed that sex is dirty and all the more enjoyable for it. Leila would be repelled when he told her, but at least he would know that the reaction was centred on him alone. He would know where he was. There would be no question of his having to stand by meekly while she found other men repugnant one night a week . . .

"Nice big room I've got for you," Betty said. "You could live there in style for only twenty a week, everything thrown in."

"*Every*thing?" Redpath did his imitation of Groucho Marx, defiantly repressing a small twinge of sadness.

"Cheeky!" She moved away from him a short distance, reassured now that he had started behaving in accordance with a recognisable norm.

Why isn't Boswell here to record this stuff for posterity? Redpath looked around the park, battling with a sense of unreality, his eyes taking in the islands of shrubbery, the young matrons with their baby carriages, the perimeter of terraced houses in the middle distance. He froze as his gaze steadied on the figure of a man who was standing in the shade of some bushes not twenty paces away. The man, who was wearing a brown boiler suit, had thick sloping shoulders and an abnormally large jutting chin. He was regarding Redpath and Betty York with a fixed, eager smile which somehow gave him the appearance of being subnormal.

"Don't look now, but I'd like your honest opinion," Redpath whispered, lowering his eyes. "Is that Igor or Quasimodo?"

As often happens when a person is told not to look around, Betty immediately turned her head. "What are you on about, love?"

Redpath looked again and was surprised to see that the odd-looking man was no longer in sight. The bushes were hardly thick enough to provide cover and he had to conclude that the man, anxious to avoid being seen, had sprinted to the cover of a tree.

Christ, I wonder is this place like this all the time? If it is, I'm going to come back with a movie camera and make the wildlife film to end all wildlife films.

"I thought we'd picked up a peeping Tom," he said.

"That's your guilty conscience." Betty exhaled a stream of smoke in his direction. "Have you got a guilty conscience, John?"

"Not yet, but I'm in the market for one."

Betty threw away her half-finished cigarette with an air of finality which caused a lurching sensation in his chest. "You'd best come and look at the room. Before you make up your mind, like. How about it?"

"Is it far?"

"Not far. Woodstock Road."

"It's far enough," Redpath said, making a token effort to draw back from the edge of the precipice. "I mean . . ."

"I can drive you there in ten minutes. Drop you in town again afterwards." Betty stood up, seemingly aiming her torso at him. The assemblage of strongly jutting breasts, low-waisted denims, leather belt and copper rivets made her look like a rodeo performer. Her black hair was deeply waved, heavy with natural oils and reached far below her shoulders.

Redpath felt a return of the raw, basic desire he had experienced earlier. *You could wreck yourself there,* he thought,

31

reverting to the terminology which had been popular among his school friends. *Wipe out your mind. Wipe out all trace of Listerine Leila and faces sculpted out of raw beef.*

He got to his feet, smiling, committed, and walked with Betty towards the park gates. A train hooted routinely in the distance and white smoke plumed up from the steelworks. As he walked, Redpath made a mental list of three possibilities relating to the woman he was with—it could be that she was simply a prostitute, and that the line about a boarding house was a defence against the police; it could be that she was a landlady with lusty appetites and no inhibitions, who believed in combining business with pleasure; and it could also be that she was a landlady, complete with hulking great husband, who used unscrupulous methods to draw in paying tenants. He was weighing up the third possibility—after all, everything she had said had been equivocal—when they reached a line of parked vehicles.

Taking a set of keys from her jacket pocket, Betty stopped at a mud-spattered grey Ford transit. "It isn't locked," she said, pointing at the passenger door.

"Right." Wondering why the van looked familiar to him, Redpath slid open the door and recoiled in shock. The man he had seen in the park, the furtive stranger with the acromegalic chin, was smiling at him from the passenger seat. Redpath stood in silence for a moment, dumbfounded.

Betty opened the door at her side and paused as she saw the front seat occupant. "What are you doing here?" she said with some exasperation, but no surprise in her voice.

"Give us a lift, Betty," the man said in a gentle, almost-melodious voice which contrasted with his uncouth appearance. "Give us a lift home."

She put her hands on her hips. "Albert, have you been following me around?"

"No, Betty, honest. I seen your van, that's all." The man made a vague gesture with enormous hands. "I just want a lift home."

"All right, but you'll have to go in the back."

"Yes, Betty, yes." The man flashed Redpath a triumphant smile and began to clamber over the back of the seat into the dark interior of the vehicle. His movements were clumsy and hampered by the lack of space and the tightness of his brown

32

boiler suit, from a side pocket of which there projected, incongruously, a pack of American cigarettes. Redpath looked away from him and stared thoughtfully in the direction of the park. The man, Albert, *had* been following Betty—who was perhaps his landlady—but an even more remarkable thing about him was that, in spite of his ungainliness, he must have had the ability to cover ground unobtrusively and with the speed of an Olympic runner. The stretch of parkland between the main gate and the place where Redpath had been sitting was fairly open, so Albert must have taken a lengthy detour and yet had managed to reach the van well ahead of its driver. It was difficult to see how the feat had been achieved at all.

"Hop in, love," Betty said, starting the engine.

Redpath frowned at the now-empty passenger seat, then got into the transit and closed the door. Betty moved the vehicle off immediately, handling the gears and steering with a rough competence. Redpath waited attentively, and several minutes passed before it dawned on him that she was neither going to introduce nor account for the extra passenger who was squatting on the layer of potato sacks, newspapers and old scraps of carpet covering the bed of the van. For his part, Albert appeared content to maintain a watchful silence.

Another searchlight on the back of my neck—this wasn't part of the deal.

Redpath stared at the swift-changing views ahead and retreated into his thoughts. As one who had purposely made the transition from one consumer group to another—a process which used to be called going up in the world or graduating from working class to middle class—he had reckoned himself to be a man of two worlds, but there were things he had forgotten. One of his most repeated jokes was that the principal difference between the working class and the middle class was that the former felt no obligation to answer letters—now he could recall a more salient characteristic. Throughout his childhood and early youth he had never seen anybody being introduced to anybody else. Redpath himself, at the age of fifteen, had met a girl, had gone out with her on three occasions for fierce necking sessions, and had parted from her without ever learning her name. It seemed on reflection that it was only in the "higher" social orders that people felt ill at ease in the company of those who had not been formally identified and labelled for them, perhaps because they had more to lose and saw strangers as a potential menace . . .

That can't be right, because I've got bugger all to lose and I don't like being cooped up in a tin box with somebody I don't know. Especially when he looks like a member of the Addams family. It's time to bale out, chum.

The van reached Calbridge's Woodstock Road, which was a redbrick canyon of aging dwellings, many of them—particularly those at intersections—converted into small shops and branch offices for banks and insurance companies. A short time later, after making a left turn and a right into narrower streets, Betty York halted the vehicle outside a tall, bay-windowed house which was near the end of a Victorian terrace. The building was a member of that vast and durable population of houses which had spread the length and breadth of the land in the previous century. Built to standards which in many ways were far superior to those of modern constructors, virtually identical in size and general layout, forming a major part of the corpus of every town and city, the class of house provided much of the accommodation for students, young couples and the elderly; supplied cheap and roomy premises for GPs, dentists, chiropodists, chiropractors, struggling architects, infant advertising agencies and the less affluent charities; provided the bulk of the work for jobbing plumbers and repairmen and woodworm eradicators; served as atmospheric settings for the most sordid scandals and the most sensational murders. It was a type of house Redpath had always hated.

He got out of the van and stood hesitantly on the footpath, taking in the house's dark brown door and window frames, the tarnished numerals 131 on the transom, the mosses which clung like caterpillars between the bricks, the patch of garden with its black but infertile soil and wisps of flattened grass. Albert went by him with a scuffling of booted feet and disappeared into the house, leaving the front door ajar. Redpath looked into the porch and experienced a strange *frisson*, a feather-flick of coolness, when he saw that the half-glazed inner door had a large amber-coloured fleur-de-lis in the centre of its leaded panes.

34

When I go inside, he thought, *there'll be a staircase ahead of me on the right, and at the top of that stair there'll be a long landing running through to the back of the house, with a window at the far end of it, and on that window there'll be another fleur-de-lis just like the one on the front door.*

"It's nice around here," Betty said, appearing at his side. "Nice and quiet. No bother, like."

Redpath looked over her head towards the semi-antique cast iron sign which was screwed to the wall of the last house in the terrace. It said: RABY STREET. The name meant nothing to him, and yet there had been an odd quality about his vision of the house's interior—a hint of poignancy, perhaps—which suggested recognition rather than prescience.

This isn't my part of the town, for God's sake. I've never been to this house before. It must be something more to do with that muck that I let Nevison and his crew shoot into me . . .

Betty took his arm, and the pliant warmth of her breast came through his sleeve. "I'll show you the room, love. It's at the back—where you get most of the sun."

Redpath allowed himself to be led forward like a child being coaxed into school on the first day. Betty opened the inner door for him and he went through into the hallway. The staircase on his right terminated in a long landing, and at the far end of the landing was a window featuring a stained glass fleur-de-lis. Rays of sunlight streaming through the window emphasised the darkness of the rest of the house. Redpath jerked his head back in alarm as his nostrils filled with an overpowering smell of cloves. The cloying aroma was gone in a second and he understood at once that it had been synaesthetic, a false sensation triggered by his seeing the house's rear window exactly as he had anticipated. He shivered, suddenly feeling that he had been given a warning.

"This way, love." Betty went up the stairs ahead of him, each step causing diagonal ripple patterns to appear in the taut denim of haunch and thigh. As he followed her to the landing he kept looking around for Albert, half-expecting to see him grinning from a doorway, but the house seemed to have absorbed the strange individual into itself. The only sound was that of their footsteps on the thinly carpeted treads as they made their way up a second flight of stairs. There were two doors on the top

35

landing, both painted an incongruous nursery pink.

Children grow up in places like this, too. God help them.

Betty opened the door which was nearer the back of the house and went ahead of Redpath into a largish square bedroom. The floorcovering was pink oilcloth heavily disfigured with parallel brown lines marking the edges of the underlying boards. Redpath advanced into the room and saw that it contained a double bed, a wardrobe, two tallboys and a dresser—all culled from old suites of differing design and employing different woods. In the middle of the ceiling was a pendant light fitting which was dragged out of plumb by the flex connecting it to a second light stapled to the wall above the bed.

"It isn't Buck House," Betty commented, "but you'll be very comfortable here, John. Bathroom's just at the foot of the stairs."

She's serious about the room, Redpath thought, walking to the window. *How am I going to get out of this?*

Below the window was the grey slate roof of the lower rear section of the house, and further down he could see an enclosed yard with brick outhouses and an old-style clothes wringer standing beside two dustbins. Beyond the yard wall was another row of three-storey houses which would have limited his field of view but for the fact that, slightly to his left, two houses had been chopped cleanly out of the terrace, possibly by a wartime bomb. Through the gap Redpath could see, as though artfully crowded into a frame, the smokestacks, gantries, spires and trees of Calbridge, all glowing with the clean light of normality, and he was seized by a yearning to be out there doing ordinary things like sitting in a coffee bar or getting his hair trimmed or taking a book back to the library. There was a creaking sound behind him and he turned to see that Betty had sat on the edge of the bed.

"Soft mattress," she said, her eyes fixed solemnly on his. "I like a nice soft mattress."

Redpath crossed the room, stood in front of her and placed his hands on her shoulders. He felt cold and ill. She tried to fall back on to the bed and draw him down on top of her, but he tightened his grip on her shoulders and stiffened his body, keeping her sitting upright.

"It's like that, is it?" she said, lowering her gaze to his belt

36

buckle which was on a level with her face. She put her hands on the buckle and began sliding the belt's leather tongue through the clasp.

Redpath stood motionless for a moment, his body a pounding column of blood, then he broke free and ran from the room, plunging down through the brown dimness of the house on nerveless legs, fleeing like a man in a nightmare and not slowing down until he was outside in the lemon-coloured sunlight of the street. He strode to the nearest corner and rounded it into the cross-street without looking back, anxious to break the visual connections with the house which he could feel clinging to him like skeins of gossamer.

CHAPTER 2

Let that be a lesson to you. Redpath walked for more than a mile intoning the same sentence over and over again, making it a kind of silent chant, his pace gradually slowing as he got further from the house in Raby Street. *Let that be a lesson to you.* Almost trembling with relief, he began loitering at shop windows and taking an interest in things which had not interested him before—the range of styles in transistor radios, the price of wallpaper, the cubic capacities of refrigerators. *Let that be a lesson to you.*

Some thirty minutes had gone by before he got the moral of the morning's escapade into sharp focus in his mind, and it concerned Leila. He could see very clearly now that he loved, admired and needed her; that picking a quarrel with her had been an act of monumental stupidity; that top priority had to be given to finding a way of patching up the relationship. Gazing intently into the window of a home bakery as though seeking significance in the arrangement of cakes and scones, he decided that getting Leila completely on her own was a tactical necessity. He had already proved the futility of trying to speak to her in the office.

It was wrong of her to laugh at me like that. Very wrong. Perhaps she needs to be taught a lesson as well. I mean, there's no bigger champion of women's lib than I am—but lib is an old word for geld. It bears thinking about . . .

Redpath looked at his watch, frowning, and calculated that if he went straight to the park and got his bicycle he could reach Leila's flat on the Leicester Road before she did. She had said she was going home only to pick up some papers, but he ought to be able to talk her into making coffee and with a little time in hand, in the undisturbed quietness of her flat, he should also be able to straighten things out. He would do everything in his power to convince her that he would be happy to get back on the old footing, that he would never be jealous or possessive again.

But is that true, John? Is it really true? If you can refuse other women, why can't she refuse other men? Why can't she learn her lesson the way you learned yours?

The sparse population of Churchill Gardens had changed when Redpath returned for his bicycle, the young matrons with their baby carriages and toddlers having been replaced by workers from the nearby steelworks and factories. There was a smell of hot food and vinegar in the air, reminding Redpath that he was hungry. He went to his bicycle, stooped to unchain it and halted in that position, staring at the torpedo-shaped combination lock. The four-digit number he had used practically every day for years was gone from his memory.

"This is stupid," he said aloud. "I *know* this number." He narrowed his eyes at the lock, making a painful effort to remember, then his fingers moved almost of their own accord and set up the combination 1–2–1–6. Without any certainty that the correct digits had been selected, he tugged on the lock and it slid apart. He got on to the bicycle and, feeling strangely chastened, rode off in the direction of Leicester Road.

Leila Mostyn's flat was on the second floor of a large detached house set back a discreet distance from the main road. Its pleasant architecture had been marred by the tacking on of a narrow brick structure containing new concrete stairs, and most of the front garden was given over to the parking of cars, but the building still retained an air of genteel exclusiveness. The first time Redpath had seen it he had been struck by how closely it matched his preconceptions of the sort of place in which Leila would choose to live.

He was thinking nostalgically about his early, too-brief halcyon period with Leila as he rode in through the front gate and dismounted in the shade of the remaining elm trees. Her cherry-coloured mini was parked in its usual place, which meant she had left the institute rather earlier than he had expected. That, he decided, was all to the good—it would be easier to talk his way into her apartment if he arrived unexpectedly on the doorstep. He propped his bicycle against a tree, turned towards the house and froze as his mind belatedly registered the presence of a green, wedge-shaped Triumph sports car beside Leila's mini. Redpath had no real interest in cars and never, for instance, looked at their plates. But he knew that each one soon borrowed a pseudo-identity from its owner, and in this case there was something familiar about the positioning of the licence holder and the faint rain-flow patterns on the windscreen and body-work. He approached the vehicle, glanced inside and saw a bundle of pink Jeavons Institute record files on the passenger seat.

Henry Nevison!

Redpath walked across to his bicycle and stood beside it for a moment with the back of a hand pressed to his forehead. The paving stones beneath his feet seemed to be rippling, as if seen through several inches of clear water.

It doesn't mean a thing. Especially, it doesn't mean that Leila and Henry are . . . Look, Leila had to come home to pick up some paperwork. Right? Urgent stuff. Papers that she should have brought in the morning—papers that Henry needs. In all probability he's going straight on to a meeting somewhere, and that's why he came home with her at lunchtime instead of wait-ing until she brought the stuff back with her in the afternoon. It's all perfectly normal and reasonable and innocent.

Who's kidding who around here?

Who, my poor deluded and ungrammatical friend, is kidding WHOM around here?

And who needs to be taught a lesson?

Redpath wheeled his bicycle to the back of the house and placed it in an inconspicuous position against a shed which was used for storing garden tools. He knelt down and began tinker-ing with the rear brake adjuster, making himself invisible from the house and at the same time providing a cover story for the benefit of anybody who might come along. There was, however, little chance of his being discovered because the house tended to be deserted at midday and the rear aspect was well screened with trellises and shrubs. The biggest risk he could think of lay in the fact that he had both curtailed his field of vision and entered a shady area where there was a noticeable drop in light intensity. Those were two potent trigger factors and, for all he knew, kneeling down—altering the blood pressure at different valves throughout his body—was another. It was when he had knelt to pick up his mail that the day had begun to go so disastrously haywire, and he was in no mood for receiving visions, telepathic or otherwise. He could do without glistening red masks and slurries of congealing blood, and he particularly did not want to see Henry through Leila's eyes or Leila through Henry's eyes if they were doing what he thought they were doing up there in the plushy, peachy noonday stillness of her bedroom.

Redpath stared down at his hands and tried to decide if they really were quivering or if there was a shimmering in his eyes.

I don't like that rippling effect. It makes everything seem unreal, like images projected on a screen. Of course, that's all the contact we have with the outside world—two little images projected on two little screens at the back of our eyes. I wonder what it's like when your retinas detach and roll up and you see the world rolling up with them, foreshortening and disappearing? Sorry, the Projectionist says. Technical hitch. That's the end of the show. You could die . . .

The booming sound of the Triumph's engine mingled with the private arterial pounding in Redpath's ears. He raised his eyes and saw the low-slung shape wheeling out on to the Leicester Road in a blinding spray of sunlight reflected from its side windows. After-images danced inside his head, circles of violet fire.

He stood up and walked quickly to the tacked-on entrance which served the flats. The white concrete treads of the stairs flickered like stroboscopes as he sprinted up them. There was no time to waste—the trick being to ring Leila's doorbell so soon after Nevison's departure that she would assume he had returned and would fling the door open without mental or physical preparation. *The truth will out.* He reached the second floor landing, with its glossy olive green door, and pressed the bellpush. There was no immediate reply. He shifted his weight from one foot to the other and back again. It was taking too long; element of surprise being lost.

The key! Where was the key she thought he knew nothing about, the one she had always hung back to conceal? Not under the doormat—that would be too obvious. Redpath lifted the single plastic flowerpot and saw there was nothing on the windowsill underneath it. In the act of replacing the pot he hesitated, struck by a new thought, and raised the pot to eye level. The key was stuck to the underside of it, held in place by a soft pad of Blu-tack. *Thinks she's clever!* He took the key, twisted it in the lock, then he was inside standing in the short hall which opened into every room in the flat. The rasping sound of his own breath added to the pulsing roar in his ears.

Leila came out of the kitchen. She was carrying a glass of milk and she was naked except for bedroom slippers and a triangle of white nylon across her hips. Her eyes and mouth widened—two white circles of fear, one pink circle of guilt—as she saw Redpath.

"John!" She tried to cover her breasts. "What are you . . ? You've no *right!*"

Redpath went towards her. "No right? Surely I've got the same rights as Henry—I mean you've got to be fair, you've got to ration it out equally. That's the liberated way, isn't it?"

"Get out of here at once."

"No chance, Leila."

"Do you want me to call the police?"

"Do they get a ration, as well?"

"*Sick!* You're so . . ." Backing away from him as she spoke, Leila suddenly turned and ran into the kitchen, throwing her glass of milk into the sink. It splintered in a blue-white fountain.

Redpath darted after her and was just in time to see her disappear through the inner door to the living-room. The telephone gave a single *ting* as she picked it up. Redpath snatched a rosewood-handled carving knife from a rack. It rippled and shimmered in his hand.

A libbing knife!

If you want libbed, my dear, I'll lib you. You've come to the right man.

He sped through into the living-room, moving as swiftly and effortlessly as though borne on the wind, and saw Leila standing at the phone with her back to him. Her back was slim, tapering, unblemished; paining him with its beauty. He ran the knife into her—striking low down, just to the right of the spine—and at the same time the force of his rush carried her down on to the settee. She gave a coughing moan and the telephone flew from her grasp. She struggled round to face him, trying to push him away, but he bore down on her with deadly fervour, using the knife again and again. Gradually the look of outrage in her eyes turned to one of astonishment, then she was no longer Leila—merely a life-sized doll staring at the ceiling in glassy pre-occupation.

There! That's what it's like to be libbed. I hope you've learned your lesson, my girl.

Redpath stood up, sneering in righteous triumph, and backed away from the settee. The telephone purred at him from the floor.

I've got to find a safer place.

He looked down at the crimson obscenities that were his hands, and a cold sense of urgency welled up inside him. Moving with a kind of post-orgasmic weakness, he went into the kitchen and began to wash his hands at the sink. The jet of cool water from the mixer tap caused a sharp stinging in his left hand and he discovered that he had managed to cut himself. There was a deep diagonal slice on the ball of the thumb which renewed the flow of blood almost as quickly as he could wash it away, infiltrating the lines of his palm. He tore a wide piece of tissue from a holder on the wall, wadded it into his left hand and hurried to the entrance of the flat. The door was still partly open. He looked out cautiously, surveying the world with the eyes of a stranger, and made sure there was nobody on the stairs or on the ground at the side of the house. Within a minute he had retrieved his bicycle and was riding in the direction of Calbridge town centre, propelling himself with long, efficient thrusts, feeling the sunlight warm on his back.

The return of sanity was like a head-on collision with an invisible barrier.

He pulled hard on both brake levers, bringing the machine to a shuddering unbalanced halt which threw him forward on to the handlebars. The chromed tubing clubbed his chest. He hunched over the front wheel, staring down at the grey-on-black mosaic of the tarmac paving, feeling his face contort into a mask of horror and disbelief. A thin rope of saliva reached tentatively downwards from his open mouth.

What have you done?
WHAT HAVE YOU DONE?

"What seems to be the trouble, sir?" The young policeman's voice was sympathetic, but he was eyeing Redpath with undisguised professional interest. His face was pink and hard, clean-shaven to the point of looking polished, the face of a man who would neither invite trouble nor go an inch out of his way to avoid it.

"What?" Redpath's gaze wandered blankly from the young officer to the nearby patrol car whose arrival he had not noticed.

"I asked if you were in trouble. Are you feeling all right?"

"I . . . I'm all right." Redpath straightened up, wiped his lips and tried to smile. "It's nothing."

"Did you come off the bike?"

"I did have a bit of a spill," Redpath said, "but I'm all right."

"Looks like you hurt your hand." The policeman's voice was less sympathetic now, and his eyes were busy. "Blood on your jacket, as well."

"I know, but it's only . . ."

"Have you got far to go, sir?"

"Not far—Bingham Terrace." *That was bloody clever,* Redpath thought, still bemused. *He was trying to find out where I live without actually asking, and I handed it to him on a plate.* "That's on Disley High Street."

"I know where it is, sir. It's right on the other side of town."

"Yes, but Calbridge is a small place, isn't it? I mean, it's not like crossing London or Los Angeles."

The policeman was not amused. "You can soon work up a thirst on a pushbike on a day like this."

"I don't drink," Redpath said, uneasily aware that the officer was not satisfied and was digging his heels in, that it was time to play the old trump card. "I'm an epileptic, you see—daren't go near booze." He was rewarded by a barely perceptible slackening of the muscles of the policeman's waxy face, a flicker of ancient fears in the eyes.

"I didn't realise that, sir."

Redpath showed his Medic-Alert bracelet in the manner of one producing a badge of authority. "It's something you learn to live with."

"How are you now?"

"Oh, I'm fine. I haven't been having one of my turns or anything like that."

"So you'll be able to get home all right on your own." The relief in the policeman's voice was unmistakable. "I mean, we could give you a lift if . . ."

"No, I'm fine. Honestly." Redpath smiled reassuringly at the policeman, watching him walk away and get into his car. He remained in the same position, standing astride the bicycle, until the car had moved off, then he became aware of a liquid warmth, stealthy and shameful, spreading down his thighs. A pool of urine made a furtive appearance beside his right shoe. He stared down at it, his vision distorted by tears.

I knew I was turning into a maniac. A frigging, homicidal, enuretic maniac. What's going to happen to me now?

A part of Redpath's mind, the part which ever held itself aloof from matters of conscience, told him that Leila's body would soon be discovered and that he would quickly be chosen as the prime suspect. Marge Rawlings would be only too pleased to testify that he knew Leila was going home at lunchtime and that he was motivated by jealousy, but her evidence was likely to be superfluous. He had left the murder weapon behind with his fingerprints all over it, and he had brought himself to the attention of the police at exactly the right time and place to link him to the crime. Short of committing the murder before an invited audience, he could not have handed the CID a more open-and-shut case. It was doubtful, considering the time it would take, if it was even prudent for him to go back to his own flat to change his clothing . . .

I've got to find a safer place!

Shocked, appalled, confused, driven by an instinctive desire to crawl into hiding, Redpath mounted the bicycle and rode off through the suburban alternation of sunlight and tree-shade, barely aware that he was heading in the direction of the house in Raby Street.

CHAPTER 3

THE DOOR WAS opened by a sleek, fat, well-groomed man who stared at Redpath with undisguised glee. "I told you it was him," the fat man called over his shoulder, projecting his voice into the back of the house. "Didn't I tell you? Didn't I tell you it was him?" The only immediate response was the muffled slamming of a door somewhere within.

"Pardon me," Redpath said, taken aback. " Is . . . Betty in?"

"Sure thing, pardner, sure thing," the fat man said breezily in a faked Hollywood cowboy accent. "Step this way." He stood aside to let Redpath enter the hall, then closed the outer door, reducing the ambient light to a whitish glow which came in through the transom. The fleur-de-lis on the half-glazed inner door seemed to deepen from amber to brown. Looking at the simplistic design Redpath again caught the scent of non-existent cloves.

"Ah . . ." He sought desperately for something to say and heard himself utter a classic banality. "Nice day."

"I'm Wilbur Tennent," the fat man said, smiling eagerly at Redpath and now speaking normally. He had the neat, very regular features that are often associated with obesity and his teeth were small and even. His smoothly-combed greying hair and light grey suit with its window-pane checks gave him something of the appearance of a successful bookmaker. To Redpath's eye he seemed quite out of place in the dark brown dinginess of the house.

"I expect Betty has told you all about me," Tennent added. "I don't usually solicit new clients—too big a waiting list, you know how it is—but I've got to make an exception in your case, John. After all, you're going to be one of the family, so to speak."

46

"Really?" Redpath gazed at the other man's snowy, gold-studded cuffs with a growing disquiet, suddenly aware of the stained and odorous condition of his own clothing. *What the hell's going on here? How does he know I'm going to be one of the family? What sort of a family would want me, anyway?*

"I've got an absolute cert in the last race at Aintree, and I'm going to give it to you for the odds of a tenner," Tennent said, smiling at Redpath with uncritical friendliness. "How's that?"

Redpath shook his head, beginning to see the light. "I haven't any money."

Tennent's smile hardly wavered. "Tell you what I'll do, John. I'll lay the bet on your behalf and I'll split the winnings with you—after taking my tenner back out, of course. Just to get you started. Now I can't say fairer than that, can I?"

"I don't gamble."

"This isn't *gambling*, John—this is shafting the bookies, making them contribute to a worthy cause. You're on Swordsmith for a tenner, right?"

"Look, I told you I don't . . ." Redpath broke off in mid-sentence, choked with annoyance and a sense of the monstrous unfairness of what was happening to him. The thing he needed most in all the world was a breathing space, a chance to hide out—even if only for a day or two—and think and come to terms with himself. Murder was a big thing, and surely to God a murderer was entitled to some reflective solitude without being hustled and pressured by every Flash Harry that came along. Redpath, suppressing an urge to run away, glanced up the first flight of stairs and saw two women watching him from the landing.

One of them was Betty York, still clad in blue velvet jacket and faded jeans, exactly as when he had first met her in the park. The other, from what he could see of her in near-silhouette, was a very tall and stooped old woman in an ankle-length dress. Her ivory-coloured hair was drawn into a bun and she wore rimless spectacles to which had been attached a safety loop of black ribbon. The overall impression was one of genteel frailty, and yet there was a subtle wrongness about her appearance which Redpath, even in his numbed condition, found slightly disturbing.

It can't be a man dressed up. It can't be Anthony Perkins

47

*getting ready to do in Janet Leigh. That would be too much—
even for this ass-hole of a place.*

"Look who it is," Betty York said, coming down the stairs to
meet him. "Have you been to collect your stuff, love?" There
was nothing in her manner to suggest that anything even faintly
out of the ordinary had occurred between them in the upstairs
room, something for which Redpath felt a profound relief.

"I haven't got any stuff," he mumbled. "Just my bicycle."

"I'll get Albert to put it round the back for you."

"Thanks."

"You're just in time, you know," Betty said, taking his elbow
and drawing him up the stairs. "There's a big demand for comfortable digs in a nice area like this. If I'd put an ad in the
Herald I could've let that room a dozen times over. At the top
rate, too."

Money, Redpath thought. *People still use that stuff called
money.*

"About the rent," he said. "I'm afraid I haven't . . ."

"Don't worry about rent, son." Tennent gave him a thumbs-up
sign and an exaggerated slow-motion wink. "Swordsmith is paying *your* rent. You'll have plenty of rent tomorrow."

"You leave the boy alone," Betty scolded. "He's not interested
in your get-rich-quick schemes. Come on, John."

Redpath nodded compliantly. *Change of role—streetwalker to
mother hen. What happened?* He followed Betty's strongly-
working haunches to the landing, turned towards the front of the
house and was just in time to see the tall old woman hurry into
the first bedroom on the right. Instead of fully closing the door
after her she remained in the narrow aperture and watched
Redpath as he went by. Her powdery face was white, the skin
like crumpled vellum.

"That's Miss Connie," Betty said in a loud voice. "Pay no
heed."

Redpath, who had been avoiding looking at Miss Connie,
glanced involuntarily in her direction and saw that the room
behind her was unexpectedly colourful, a patchwork of bright-
hued rectangles interspersed with metallic glitters. The image
was lost to him before he had time to interpret it, but as he
turned on to the upper stair it came to him that Miss Connie's

room was piled high with canned foodstuffs, enough to stock a modest-sized store. There had even been cartons sitting on the bed, and the very air in the vicinity smelt like a grocer's shop— bacon, coffee, oranges, washing powder.

Perhaps it really is a shop. Remember old Mrs Crangle who set up a counter in her own living-room and sold toffee apples across it? And Gus Minihan who tried to turn his garage into a speak-easy selling home-brewed ale? But it ought to be in the front room downstairs . . .

"Here we are, love." Betty stopped at the door of the rear bedroom on the top floor and turned to face Redpath. She was breathing deeply after the climb, her ample breasts lifting against the crimson material of her T-shirt. Redpath noted the phenomenon with a wan detachment and reached for the door handle, anxious to get into the room and lock the door and find out who he was.

Betty looked down at his hand. "Are you hurt?"

"It's nothing. I sliced it on a piece of glass."

"I can get some plaster from Miss Connie."

"No, it's all right. I'm a bit tired, that's all. I'd like to lie down for a while." Redpath went into the room and was relieved to see that Betty was making no move to come in with him. "If I can get my head down for a couple of hours I'll come and talk to you about the rent and so forth. Okay?"

Betty nodded and gave him a sympathetic smile. "Are you in some kind of trouble, love?"

"What makes you say that?" Redpath tried to look indignant.

"You'll be all right here, love. Nobody can find you here."

"Thanks." Redpath closed the door and stood turning his head from side to side in an upsurge of panic. *That can't be customary, damn it all! If there's a handbook of etiquette for landladies it doesn't say, 'Put new guests at ease by telling them they're safe from the law.'*

What is this place? What am I DOING here?

He surveyed the room—taking in the brown-ruled pink oil-cloth, the mismatching furniture, the cobbled-up lighting arrangement—and went to the single window. The only change in the view outside was a slight difference in the angle of the shadows. As before, the notch in the screening row of houses provided a

49

compressed view of Calbridge, and as before he found something tremendously endearing in the diorama of sunlit rooftops and spires—but now the town and the cosy normality it represented seemed distant and unreachable. There could be no more drowsing in coffee bars, reading dog-eared week-end magazines in the barber shop, taking books back to the stuffy, sane sanctuary of the public library . . .

He gripped the central cross-member of the window and leaned his weight on it, almost hoping it would give way. The window shifted slightly and a small piece of paper which had been wadded into the frame, probably to prevent vibration, fell on to the sill. He absent-mindedly picked up the paper, unfolded it and saw that it was a scrap of stationery with the heading, *Commodore Hotel, Hastings, Sussex.* His eyes mechanically scanned the words which had been written on it with a green felt-tip pen:

Keratin is a tough fibrous protein containing much sulphur, occurring in the epidermis of vertebrates, forming resistant outermost layer of skin, and also hair, feathers, horny scales, nails, claws, hooves and outer coating of horns of cows, sheep, etc. This means that, weight for weight, a bird is probably a better

Redpath stared moodily at the incomplete text, resenting its lack of relevance to anything which concerned him, then crumpled up the paper. He turned and threw himself down on the bed, burying his face in the pillows.

"I'm so sorry, Leila," he whispered. "I'm sorry about being possessive, I'm sorry I called you Listerine, I'm sorry I put that libbing knife into you . . . Leila! *Leila!*"

The bad dream started off as a low-key affair, a Class Two nightmare.

Redpath, who was something of an expert on bad dreams, had devised his classification system when he was still a youth. Class One nightmares were the worst, the mind-quakers, the soul-rapers, the sort from which he sometimes woke up screaming, to spend the rest of the night reading newspapers in the kitchen, well aware of the fact that it would be unsafe to go back to sleep because his subconscious had been affected by a ghastly contamination which only the morning sun could disperse. The thing which made a Class One nightmare so terrible, Redpath understood, was that it did not manifest itself as a nightmare—he would be led into it in a state of vulnerability, deceived into believing that its events were the events of the real world.

A Class Two nightmare could have the same type of dreadful scenario, but here a kind of psychological double-think would be in evidence, and Redpath would *know* the circumstances were imaginary and thus be protected. He could stroll through a Class Two, taking a detached and almost academic interest in the shadow play, undeniably afraid—but in the pleasurable, controllable way he had known as a small boy watching a horror show in the cinema, where it was always possible to turn one's eyes away from the screen and study the orange-glowing exit signs and the details of the roof architecture.

In the present instance, he found himself standing on the stairs of the house in Raby Street, looking down into the hall, and he knew he was dreaming because the hall floor was all wrong. It was much too wide and spacious, and instead of being covered with brown linoleum it was made up of large pale green and biscuit-coloured tiles embossed with a leaf pattern in low relief. It was, quite obviously, the floor of the entrance hall of the psychophysiology building at the Jeavons Institute.

This could be a bad bit!

Redpath tensed himself apprehensively as he remembered the vision he had had that morning, the wash of clotted blood surging slowly in his direction, but the floor remained bright and clean. Something else was happening though. Some of the floor tiles were turning blue and becoming transparent, like slabs of amethyst, and it seemed that there were lights underneath. Small things were moving down there, under the floor.

Strange! Unease-making, but not frightening. Very strange!

He turned away and found himself on the landing, moving towards the rear window with its yellow fleur-de-lis. There were two doors on his left—bathroom and separate toilet. There was one door on his right—Albert's bedroom. The door was slightly ajar. He looked into the room and saw that Albert, fully clad in his brown boiler suit and heavy work boots, was sleeping on the bed. Not actually *on* the bed, however. He was floating in the air about three inches above the coverlet and daylight was clearly

51

visible beneath his body. His enormous hands twitched slightly in his sleep.

Curiouser and curiouser!

Redpath was back on the stairs now and going down into the hall, which had resumed its normal aspect. The house was very quiet, as though Albert and he were the only two in it. Where was Betty? In the kitchen? He reached the ground floor, walked six paces to the kitchen and opened the door. The long room was deserted, dishes stacked in the crazed porcelain sink, refrigerator gurgling introspectively in the corner. On his right was another door which was painted an incongruous fire-engine red. Definitely not the sort of colour one used in a kitchen. What was in there? A pantry?

Redpath felt himself drawn to the door, was compelled to open it. On the other side was a flight of stone steps leading down into the darkness of a cellar.

Hey, I'm starting not to like this. It's getting too real. Can a Class Two escalate-degenerate into a Class One?

Redpath walked down the stone steps, advancing one foot slowly past the other. He was breathing noisily now, caught in the grip of an unmanning fear, and yet unable to turn back. The absence of light made it difficult to tell where the steps ended and the cellar floor began.

Be ready to run, that's the main thing. Be poised. At the first sign of movement—even if it's only a mouse—run like the wind, and that way you'll be safe. Fear lends you wings, you know.

He paused on the last dimly-visible step, waiting for his eyes to adjust to the darkness. The cellar was warmer than he had expected and the air in it was heavy. Heavy, sweet and sickening . . .

Be poised!

Redpath turned his head, straining his eyes to pick up a movement, and when the movement came he discovered that it had been with him all along and he had failed to notice it because he had been watching out for a small localized movement, an individual movement, and what had been happening all the time was that the walls and ceiling and floor of the cellar had been moving. They were dark red in colour, and they were glistening, and they had been gently palpitating, heaving with anticipation. And now they were reaching towards him, reaching out with shapeless arms . . .

My God, the whole cellar is a stomach!
I'VE WALKED INTO THE HOUSE'S STOMACH!

Redpath was rescued by the sound of his own moaning, the inarticulate, deep-chested, slack-throated expression of the ultimate fear. He awoke to find himself lying face downwards on the bed, mildly asphyxiated by his own breath, making vague little swimming movements with his arms and legs. The room was warm and intensely bright, filled with the sun's cleansing radiance.

It had only been a nightmare, he realised, but where was that beautiful sense of relief? At this stage he should have been luxuriating in the checked, confirmed and authorised knowledge, officially approved and rubber-stamped, that people like Stanley Laurel, Albert Schweitzer and Richmal Crompton were secure on their thrones and all was right with the world. But the weight of dread had not lifted; it had merely shifted . . .

Leila! I killed Leila! I'm not the person I always believed myself to be. I'm a murderer!

Redpath moaned again, quietly this time, moved to the side of the bed and sat with his elbows on his knees, face supported in his hands. In that position he could see through a truncated tunnel formed by his palms and fingers, and his eyes came to focus on a small section of powder blue carpet between his feet. He stared at it for perhaps twenty seconds before accepting the fact that it *was* a powder blue carpet and not the pink oilcloth which had covered the floor when he had entered the bedroom a short time earlier.

What the . . ?

Redpath raised his head and looked around the room, his eyes widening as he found that everything was different. There was a built-in fitment instead of the old-fashioned wardrobe he remembered, and the other furniture was of a more modern design, unified and painted white. The overhead light was now a plastic dome which clung to the ceiling like a giant limpet. Most disturbing of all, however, was the change which had come over the quality of the sunlight streaming in through the window.

53

It was morning sunlight—and when he had lain down on the bed the time had been late afternoon.

Redpath's shoulders slumped as he deduced what must have happened. At breakfast time that morning, away back in his previous existence, he had omitted to take his daily shot of Epanutin, thereby laying himself open to the threat of an attack. And the subsequent chain of events hardly squared with the sort of calm, orderly way of life which was recommended for the control of epilepsy. Under those circumstances it was in the cards for him to experience a break in continuity, to regain consciousness in strange surroundings. It had happened to him before and it would happen again and again if he neglected to . . .

The questions hit him simultaneously, like a swarm of shotgun pellets.

If he had had an attack, why should other people in the house have taken the trouble to move him to a different room?

If he had had an attack, where was the usual aftermath of headache, bodily pain and confusion?

If he had had an attack and had drifted from unconsciousness into a lengthy sleep, why did he feel that he had lain down only a few minutes ago?

Where *was* everybody?

Redpath—driven by a formless suspicion—stood up and walked to the window. He parted the screening curtains of white lace and stood for a moment, rigid with shock, as his disbelieving eyes took in the details of what lay beyond.

The view was totally unfamiliar to him.

He was looking down on a roughly triangular area bounded by rows of tall houses built of sandstone—a constructional material he could not reconcile with the Woodstock Road district of Calbridge. Throughout the area was a hodgepodge of garages, outhouses, walls, corrugated iron fences, clothes lines, telephone poles and parched trees. Two large saloon cars were partially visible in the midst of the clutter, apparently abandoned. Above the rooftops and television aerials was a sky which looked stratospheric in its dark blue clarity.

I'm not even in the same house! I'm not even in the same PLACE!

Redpath released the curtain and pressed the back of a hand to his lips.

I must have been out cold for hours, after all, and they must have taken me somewhere while I didn't know what was going on, perhaps out of Calbridge altogether, and for all I know they thought I was dead and for all I know they might have dumped me somewhere and they'd no right to treat me like that . . . NO RIGHT AT ALL!

Redpath strode to the bedroom door, flung it open and went out onto a landing, deliberately making a great deal of noise with his feet.

"Anybody there?" he shouted into the stairwell, noting as he did so that the house was very similar in its general layout to the one in Raby Street. "Is anybody at home?"

The silence was complete except for faint traffic sounds filtering in from the street. He hesitated, looking around him, absorbing the curious fact that the location of the room he had just left—top rear in a three-storey dwelling—corresponded exactly with that of his room in the other house. The realisation brought with it a stabbing of unease and self-doubt. Could it be that he was almost totally confused? Could it be that he was actually in the same house as before, and that his preconceptions about the bedroom furniture and the view from the window were memories transplanted from some other time and place? No previous attack, not even a *grand mal,* had ever left such a degree of disorientation in its wake—but who was to say what effects Nevison's cursed Compound 183 might have on a brain that was already being ravaged by neural storms?

Chastened, his anger subsiding, Redpath went down to the next landing. It extended through to the back of the house and terminated at a narrow window, the pebbled glass of which bore no design. Did the absence of the fleur-de-lis prove anything? Redpath thought it might, but he found it difficult to decide what the significance could be.

He continued down to the ground floor, turned back towards the room he believed to be the kitchen and tapped lightly on its door. There was no reply. He pushed open the door and paused on the threshold while he took in details of the long room with its array of sage-green fitted cupboards. The sink was a modern stainless steel affair instead of semi-antique porcelain, and the refrigerator was much larger and standing in a different corner—more points of disagreement with the house in Raby Street. It looked as though . . .

Wait a minute, dumbo! You never saw the kitchen of the other house. You got all that stuff about the old sink and the position of the fridge from your latest nightmare!

Try to get a grip on yourself!

Redpath turned his head to the right and saw—in exactly the location predicted by his nightmare—another door which could have led into a pantry or down to a cellar. He blinked at it, feeling a touch of coolness on the nape of his neck. The door itself was completely different—a patent folding model of white plastic segments in place of the bright red panelled slab of wood he had visualised—but there was something eerie about finding it in that precise location. He put out his hand, caught the slim chromium handle and slid the door aside. Beyond it was a flight of concrete steps leading down into the darkness of a cellar.

Redpath advanced helplessly to the topmost step. The air which billowed up around him from the blackness was too warm. Stale and heavy. His shuttling eyes picked out a whitish blur on the wall close beside him and he identified it as a light switch. He depressed the toggle of the switch and nothing happened, then he realised it was already in the down position. That could mean that the power was already on and that the cellar light was broken, or that the switch had been amateurishly wired upside down. A third possibility—that the switch was part of a two-way circuit—flicked into his mind and was immediately dismissed.

You can't tell me, old son, that anybody in his right mind would want a facility whereby he could go down into a spider-haunted crypt and switch the lights off while he was still down there.

Investigating the second possibility, Redpath tried pushing the toggle upwards. It moved easily, and a fluorescent brilliance pulsed into being at the bottom of the steps. He went half-way down the steps and sank on to his heels to give himself a view of the entire cellar. The square room had smooth concrete walls and floor, and it was quite bare, devoid of all the lumber and discarded possessions that Redpath expected to find in a basement. The only contents he could see were perhaps a dozen dark red, fist-sized objects scattered around the floor.

Prompted by a blend of curiosity and masochism, Redpath completed his descent into the cellar and hunkered down to examine the nearest of the small shapes. It was a bird, possibly a pigeon, which looked as though it had been sandpapered to death. The plump little body was intact as far as its musculature was concerned, but all traces of feathers and skin had been cleanly removed. Redpath's mouth twitched as he saw that even the beak and claws were missing, and for an instant the apparition he had glimpsed through the spy-hole at breakfast time—the face sculpted in redly-oozing beef—hovered at the edge of his perception.

It's time to get out of this place.

He stood up and walked backwards until the nosing of the first step was pressed against his ankles, then he turned and sprinted up the treads towards the kitchen. He had almost reached the white plastic door when it riffled its segments, as though they were feathers on an enormous wing, and partially slid across to bar his way. Without taking time to think, Redpath brushed the door aside, plunged through into the kitchen and almost immediately was out in the hall.

That door must have a faulty catch or something like that, a spring-loaded return mechanism which sticks and delays the action. I mean, I know I'm a murderer and deserve everything that's coming to me, but there has to be a limit . . .

He reached the front door, which was half-glazed with plain glass, wrenched it open and hurried out to the street, casting about for a landmark which would give him some idea of where he was. The street offered all its tiredness and shabbiness up to the morning light, like a very old tramp trying to gain free nourishment by sun-bathing, but that was its only similarity to Raby Street or any other part of urban Calbridge. Redpath looked at the brown sandstone façades, the short flights of broad steps leading up to the entrances, the unfamiliar design of the lamp standards—and was forced to accept the fact that he had no knowledge of his whereabouts. He could have been abducted to almost any part of the country.

Evidence, he thought, as ruddy sparks of indignation and

outrage began to glow far down in the dark tangles of his mind. *If I ever have to give evidence about this I want to get it right. I'm a murderer and I may deserve everything that's coming to me—but that's no reason to let the Gypsy Queen and her pals get away with a thing like this.*

He turned and looked for the number of the house he had just left, and saw a diagonal row of metal digits screwed to the pale blue door—2224. Slightly surprised by the magnitude of the number—he had never known house numbers to rise above the low hundreds—Redpath directed his attention towards a massy metallic object which was projecting upwards from the edge of the footpath beside him. The letters GFD were embossed on its green-painted surface. He stared at the object for a moment, perplexed, before identifying it as an American-style fire hydrant, a piece of street furniture which was known to him only through imported movies.

Admonishing himself not to be distracted by trivia, Redpath set off towards the nearest intersection in search of the street's name-plate. He had passed three parked cars before it dawned on him that there had been something unusual in their size and styling.

That's odd—three American jobs in the one street. Don't tell me Billy Graham's here again!

Perhaps there's a foreign car club in the area . . .

There were four more large saloon cars parked between Redpath and the intersection and, his awareness of them suddenly heightened, he noted in advance that all were of American design, sleek and roomy vehicles such as he only saw on television. Cannon cars, Rockford cars, Kojak cars. The licence plates of the first three proclaimed that they were from Illinois; the fourth was from Iowa. Bemused, drugged by the heat and the intense sunlight, Redpath reached the corner and looked up at the street sign. It said: 13 AVE S.E.

That's another weirdo. You'd almost think . . .

Redpath's thought processes ground to a shuddering halt as he glanced along the cross-street he had reached. It was a major thoroughfare which dwindled into the distance in a perfectly straight line, aiming at a remote blue mountain which was deckled with snow and which was totally unlike anything he had ever seen in Britain. Telescoped into that single perspective was a seemingly endless series of buses, cars and trucks, all of American design, all driving on the right-hand side of the road.

You'd almost think this was . . .

The sign above the small shop on the corner said, Gruber's Delicatessen, and its window was almost completely blanked off with hand-printed offers of food bargains. The prices were quoted in dollars and cents. Next to the delicatessen was a bar named Pete's Palace, which had a half-curtained window and a small neon tube advertising Budweiser. Men and women walking past Redpath wore clothing which was different to the clothing he was accustomed to seeing in Calbridge, or even London—not very different, but unmistakably different.

You'd almost think this was the United States!

Redpath pressed the heels of his hands to his temples and swayed from side to side, staring at the incomprehensible scene through slitted eyes. An elderly woman in a yellow one-piece suit halted nearby, regarded him suspiciously for a few seconds and then hurried on her way, lips moving silently.

" Can I talk to you, please?" Redpath said, going after her. She broke into a scampering run without looking back at him. He quickened his pace for two strides, then realised he was being watched by a pudgy, grey-suited man who was leaning against the window of the bar. Redpath changed course and approached the man, who was about fifty and had an irregular pattern of black and white stubble on his cheeks. The man eyed him with a mixture of uneasiness and derision.

"Where is this place?" Redpath said.

"Don't you know?" The man spoke with what Redpath took to be an American accent.

"Look, I need help—can you tell me where I am?"

"You need help, that's for goddamn sure." The man shot a knowing grin to a nonexistent companion. "What sort of stuff you trippin' out on, anyway?"

"I'm lost—that's all. Where am I?" Redpath brought his hands down from his temples and closed them into fists.

The man's grin faded. "Gilpinston."

"Gilpinston what? Gilpinston where?"

At that moment a taller and younger man with a folded

59

newspaper under his arm came out of the bar and positioned himself beside the first, a questioning expression on his face. His presence seemed to embolden the pudgy man.

"What are you hangin' round me for? Go pick on somebody else."

"I only asked you . . ." Redpath exhaled sharply, faced the younger man and made himself smile. "Do you mind if I look at your newspaper? Just for a second."

"Get lost." The younger man turned his back on Redpath and began to discuss horse racing odds with his companion. Frustration and anger seared through Redpath as though a furnace door had been flung open in his mind. He swore and grabbed the newspaper at the precise instant in which its owner decided to withdraw it from under his arm, and an absurd tug-of-war ensued for a few seconds. It ended when the pudgy man, his panda-pattern face working with indignant fury, closed in and kneed Redpath in the groin. Redpath, folding up around the centre of pain, found himself now clinging to the newspaper for support. It tore easily and he dropped to his knees, dimly aware that a number of passers-by were pausing to watch what was happening. The pudgy man, assuming the guise of a disinterested observer, moved back a few paces with his hands in his pockets. Redpath looked up at a tear-distorted world of unsympathetic giants.

"What's the matter with that guy?" a man said. "Is he sick?"

"Stoned out of his gourd, if you ask me."

"Is he English? Say, he isn't one of those characters that moved into the Rodgers' house around the corner, is he?"

"Somebody send for the cops."

"No . . ." Redpath focused his gaze roughly in the direction of the last speaker, intending to reassure him that the police would not be necessary, but by some fluke of perception he picked out a more distant and oddly familiar figure in a brown boiler suit. The man, who had an abnormally large chin and hands, was standing at the street corner, well clear of the little knot of spectators, but he was staring in Redpath's direction and his whole attitude was suggestive of furtive anxiety.

"Albert?" Redpath struggled to his feet and forced his way through a barricade of bodies. The corner was deserted. He ran to the intersection, looked along the street from which he had emerged a short time earlier, expecting to see a fleeing brown figure. The street was empty except for some small children absorbed in games. Redpath frowned, trying to think amid a tidal interplay of pain, nausea and shock. Could Albert—assuming it had been Albert he had seen—have reached the house so quickly? Could he have travelled a hundred yards in the time it took Redpath to cover fifteen?

"Where are you goin', fella?" somebody called out behind him.

"It's all right," Redpath mumbled. "It's all right." Clutching his lower abdomen with both hands, he ran towards the house along a sunlit footpath which seemed to be rocking like the deck of a ship. He had a hazy impression that he was being pursued. He reached the house in which he had found himself earlier, identified it almost by instinct, and lurched up the steps. The front door was slightly ajar. He ran into the hall, slammed the door behind him and locked it, all the while breathing in raucous gasps. The house was as quiet and lifeless as before.

"*Albert!*" His voice was that of a demented stranger. "Where are you, sneaky little bastard?"

Redpath dragged his left shoulder along the wall until he reached the first interior door and threw it open. The living-room beyond was empty, its deep armchairs brooding in introspective silence. The next room, furnished with a long table and upright chairs, also was empty of people. Redpath paused, trying to control his breathing. From where he stood he could see that there was nobody in the kitchen, and as for the cellar . . . well, he had already been in the cellar and had no wish to go back to it. The pain in his groin was getting worse, threatening to engulf his consciousness. He turned back, still cradling his genitals with both hands, ran to the foot of the stairs and made the long, long climb to the first landing. The section of the landing which extended to the back of the house had one door on the right, two on the left. The door on the right was the one which, in his nightmare, had led into Albert's bedroom. He pushed it open and groggily surveyed the deserted room, with its single bed which had not been slept upon. He backed out and crossed the landing to the nearer door on the other side. Smallest room in the house—nothing in there but a toilet pedestal. He walked three unsteady paces to the next door and swung it away from him. Bathroom. He was looking down into the tub. It contained two hideously blackened human bodies—one of them possibly that of a woman. And they looked as though they had been sandpapered to death . . .

Oh, no!

Oh, Christ Jesus . . . NO!

The world tilted away from underneath Redpath in a yawning, sickening, screaming slide which nothing could prevent. He hit the floor in a limp bundle, consciousness fleeing fast, the window at the end of the landing rippling and glimmering in his vision. A yellow fleur-de-lis unfurled its petals across the pane, like a bird of prey making ready to fly. Redpath blinked at it, all thought obliterated by dread, and discovered there were other people with him on the landing, blocking the light.

They were all there with him, smiling down at him.

Betty York, the Gypsy Queen; tricky, elusive Albert; queer old Miss Connie; plump, snowy-cuffed Wilbur Tennent, the benevolent tipster.

They were all three with him.

Smiling down at him.

Redpath closed his eyes and tried to die.

CHAPTER 4

"ARE YOU SURE I can't give you a lift?" Henry Nevison opened the door of his apple-green sports car and paused before getting in. "Leicester Road is practically on my way home."

Leila Mostyn shook her head. "Thanks, Henry, but I've one or two bits of shopping to do. I can manage better on the bus."

"Do you think your car will be all right in the morning?"

"It should be. I phoned my service station and they said they'd gone round after lunch and put in a new battery."

"Right, but if you've still got problems give me a buzz and I'll call for you in the morning."

"Thank you." Leila watched Nevison insinuate himself into the low-slung metal shell, briefly wondering why a man of his age and status should have chosen such an inappropriate style of car. Even she, who was considerably younger than Nevison and a good six inches shorter, had found it difficult to get into and out of the Triumph with anything approximating grace when she had borrowed it at lunchtime. Driving it to her flat to collect the half-yearly comparison charts she had left behind had been a demanding experience which made her yearn for the sloppy comfort of her own runaround. The obvious explanation was that Henry Nevison was trying to regain his youth, but she had learned to distrust facile *Woman's Own*-type psychology. Human beings were too complicated for that type of analysis, as anybody who had met, say, John Redpath could testify . . .

The thought of Redpath caused Leila to glance around and note that his bicycle was not in its usual place, which meant he had gone home early. She frowned as she remembered how far she had let herself be provoked by him in the morning. The remarks she had made in the presence of Marge Rawlings had been prime and unforgivable examples of schoolgirl bitchiness, but that was part of the trouble with John Redpath—he was so absurdly vulnerable that merely being near him created breaches in her own defences.

Nevison's car went by with a churning of deep gravel. Leila waved in response to his rather kingly salute and made her way out to the institute's main entrance. The double gates had been newly painted green, with the wrought iron scrollwork picked out in gold which glistened like the real thing in the late afternoon sunlight. Looking at them, Leila felt a pang of nostalgia for the uncomplicated days of her childhood, days when it had always been midsummer or Christmas, when a walk to the park had been an expedition to the far side of a cosy world, with the homely aromas of spice cakes and lavender to greet the returning traveller. In those days there had been no problems with independence or career structure or sex . . .

This is ridiculous, she almost said aloud. *I have no problems with sex—and no bicycle-riding, freckle-faced red squirrel is going to pose me any, either.*

Concentrating her thoughts on a mental shopping list, she crossed the road and walked for five minutes to reach a small local co-operative where she bought bread, yoghurt, onion salt and bleach. Another brief walk brought her to one of the Y-junctions which enabled Calbridge's spray of radial roads to send nourishing offshoots into its various suburbs. The first Leicester Road bus which came along was almost empty—it was a little too early for the daily exodus from the town centre—and she took a seat near the passenger exit. Buildings, trees and hedges began to move past the windows in a jerky progression, deflecting her thoughts inwards.

It had been a mistake to get involved with John in the first place, because he was—in the nicest possible way, and through no fault of his own, and with no hard feelings or thought of recrimination on her part—a born loser. He seemed to set himself up to be a loser by, with unerring suicidal instinct, trying to be all things he could never be. He strove to be sophisticated when he was incurably naïve, to be cosmopolitan when he was a pie-and-peas provincial, to be—using one of the movie-culture metaphors of which he was so fond—Bogart when he was Bambi. Possessor of neither money nor prospects, John Redpath had only two things going for him, and all the world knew that courage and a sense of humour were not nearly enough. Discussion closed.

When the bus reached her stop Leila descended and walked slowly to the house where she lived, the paper bag of provisions balanced on her right hip. Her car was sitting in the parking space with a folded-up garage bill tucked under one of the windscreen wipers. She removed the bill, crammed it into the pocket of her cardigan and went up the stairs towards her flat. There was a greenhouse heat in the narrow stairwell and she made up her mind to have a shower as soon as she put the milk in the refrigerator. Reaching the middle landing she paused at her own door, key in hand, staring at the other key which somebody had left projecting from the lock.

Visitor or intruder? Friend or foe?

She set the paper bag on the windowsill beside her, lifted the plastic flowerpot and felt underneath it. The spare key was gone, but—now that she thought about it—that piece of intelligence was of no immediate practical value. There was no way of telling if the key had been used by a perceptive burglar or someone to whom she had revealed its existence, nor could she predict whether or not that person had already gone away or was inside the flat waiting for her.

Leila turned the key and pushed the door wide open. She stood for a moment on the threshold, listening, then advanced cautiously into the short hall. The air in the apartment whispered with its quietness. With growing reassurance she looked into the living-room, noting that none of her possessions was missing or disarranged, then quickly checked out the other rooms. The flat was empty, which probably meant that one of her friends—it could have been any of half-a-dozen people—had made an impromptu visit and had left without remembering to return the key to its hiding place.

She went back out to the landing, retrieved the bag of provisions and brought them into the kitchen. Next, as a preliminary to undressing, she went around all the windows and adjusted the slats on the venetian blinds to an angle at which they still admitted light while obscuring the view from outside. The window in the living-room was last. She turned away from it,

C 65

already removing her cardigan, and rocked to a standstill as she glanced down at the settee. One of the cushions had been cut to shreds by a carving knife which was still projecting from it and, to lend a final touch of grisliness, the gut-like protrusions of cotton were blotched with the redness of blood.

Fingers moving uncertainly towards her mouth, Leila backed away from the settee and circled the perimeter of the room until she was standing at the kitchen door. Her perceptions were heightened and altered now, and when she looked into the kitchen she at once saw traces of blood at the sink and on the roll of absorbent tissue mounted on the wall. She went through the kitchen, choosing a central course as though to touch anything would be to risk contamination, and stopped at the telephone in the hall. Her mathematician's memory for numbers came to her aid and she was able to put a call through to Calbridge police station without using the directory.

"I'd like to speak to Detective Sergeant Pardey," she said when the call was answered, keeping her voice firm. There was a lengthy, sputtering delay during which it occurred to her that the inspection she had made of the apartment had been fairly perfunctory. She had not, for example, looked under the bed in her room, nor had she opened any wardrobe or closet doors. The thought, having gained entry to her mind, refused to be dismissed. She pressed her back to the wall, hemmed in by surroundings that suddenly seemed alien, and waited until she heard Pardey's familiar voice on the line.

"Frank? This is . . ." She swallowed, regaining the precious steadiness of tone. "This is Leila Mostyn. Can you help me, please?"

Pardey gave an exaggerated sigh. "Leila, if I've told you this once I've told you it a thousand times—once a parking ticket has been written there's nobody, not even God Almighty, who can do anything about it."

"It isn't about parking, and you know it," Leila replied, half-smiling, comforted by Pardey's habit of repeating the same ponderous witticism year in and year out.

"Well, if it's a leaky tap or a . . ."

"Frank, I've just got home from work and somebody has been in the flat."

"Oh?" Pardey's voice changed. "Anything missing?"

"I don't think so."

"Then how did you . . ? Has the place been turned over?"

"Not really." Leila described what she had found, beginning with the discovery of the key in the door and mentioning the strong possibility that the intruder was known to her.

"Do you think it was some kind of a sick joke?"

"I choose my friends more carefully than that," Leila said impatiently.

"All right. Don't touch anything—I'll get a patrol car there in a couple of minutes."

"Frank, I was hoping we could do this without any . . . fuss. I didn't want to make it official at this stage."

"You mean you don't want uniformed bobbies tramping all over the place and starting the neighbours off."

"Well, I . . ."

"And you'd like me to stop work on more important matters and give you personal VIP treatment?"

Leila made her voice small. "I suppose that's what I did want. I'm sorry."

"Think nothing of it, my little *Rostkartoffel*—that's what friends are for," Pardey said with a joviality which might have been designed to put Leila at ease. "As I said before, don't touch anything. I'll be there in a few minutes. See you."

She replaced the phone's handset and looked about her, trying to decide what should be done next. This would be a good time to check inside those wardrobes and closets, but—something for which she was grateful—Frank had told her not to touch anything. She went to the outer end of the hall and stepped out on to the small concrete landing, leaving the apartment door open behind her. From the lonely vantage point the suburb of Calbridge was predominantly green, in shades which had already begun to grow deeper with the approach of evening, looking less like a typical Midlands town and more like the environment of her parents' house near Reading. For a moment she felt a rare yearning to be at home, where her mother and father would undoubtedly be tending their lawns and flower beds. The vision of domestic security was sundered by an incursive memory of John Redpath, who claimed he hated gardening, making one of his pseudo-Wildean comments about the cultivation of lawns. *There is something ineffably sad in the spectacle of the planet's highest animal form devoting all its time and energy to the welfare of the planet's lowest vegetable form.* For an instant she could almost see him, with his spare figure and foxy coloration, declaiming, going on to belabour the point. *It makes you wonder who's the smartest.*

That was John trying to be flip and unorthodox, but underneath it all he was desperately conventional and, although he had never put his feelings into words, would have been very content to marry her and settle down to raise a crop of children and fescue grasses. And that was a fate which she, having escaped one close-mown plot of suburbia, was determined to avoid. If marriage became inevitable she was going to seek maximum recompense in terms of money, world travel, and homes that were either in the city or in the country and not somewhere in between and thus forcing her to be a circumscribed, in-between person . . .

It occurred to Leila that, in spite of her resolution, she was again devoting too much thought to John Redpath. It was a habit which should be overcome. She leaned on the window sill and stared down at the gateway of the house, waiting for Frank Pardey's car to appear and gradually becoming aware that he was taking longer to show up than she had expected. More than twenty minutes had elapsed before his unremarkable grey saloon halted on the road outside. Pardey got out and came towards the house. He was a big fair-haired man in his late thirties, with heavy shoulders and a trick of walking with a very short, knee-lifting stride as if marking time to an unseen military band.

"Sorry about the delay," he said, reaching the landing. "How are you, Leila? Not letting this throw you, I hope." He kissed her lightly on the cheek and stood back smiling, which was as close as he ever came to trying to introduce a physical element into their relationship. Leila knew he was a divorcee who disported himself to a fair extent on the local party circuit, but he was also intuitive enough to know that she saw him purely as a friend.

"I'll be all right—it's just that . . ." She pulled her cardigan

68

tighter around her and shivered slightly. "Nothing like this has ever happened to me before."

"Let's have a look at what we've got here," Pardey said encouragingly, like a dentist about to examine a troublesome tooth. He went into the flat, followed by Leila, and turned left to go directly into the living-room. She stood beside him as he knelt at the settee and closely inspected the ruined cushion and protruding knife.

"Well, he's certainly messed that up for you," he said after a few seconds. "Does the knife belong here?"

"Yes, it's one of the set that hangs in the kitchen."

"I see." Pardey stood up and gave Leila a look which she found strangely speculative. "What do you call that sandy-haired chap you came to Vicki Simpson's party with a couple of months ago? Was it Redmayne? Something like that?"

"Redpath. John Redpath." She gave an uncertain laugh. "What has that got to do with anything?"

"Does he live on the far side of town, on Disley High Street?"

"Yes, but . . ."

"He was here today. Just after one o'clock."

"How could you know that?"

"I have my methods." Pardey tried to look enigmatic. "Actually, before I came out here just now I checked with the patrol car that was covering the district earlier on, just in case they'd seen anything out of the ordinary. That's the way we get some of our best results, you know. The constable said he spoke to a man answering Redpath's description only about a quarter of a mile from here. He was riding a bicycle and he was wearing a Medic-Alert bracelet that said he was an epileptic. Is Redpath an epileptic?"

"Yes." Leila found she disliked hearing John referred to by his surname. "There's no law against that, is there?"

Pardey took the hint. "I'm sorry, Leila. I know he's a friend of yours—but if he's going to do this sort of thing . . ." His gaze flicked towards the cushion.

"What makes you think he had anything to do with this?"

"He had blood on his hands and on his jacket, quite a lot of it, and he was acting a bit strange. And I'll bet you anything you like his fingerprints are all over that knife."

Leila tried to picture John Redpath roaming around her empty apartment with a knife in his hand and her imagination baulked—he could be jealous and childishly spiteful as a result of it, but violence, even symbolic violence, simply was not his style.

"I'm sorry, Frank," she said firmly, "that doesn't make much sense to me."

Pardey moved to the window and stood looking out. "There are some questions I have to ask people so often I wish I could get them printed on conversation lozenges."

"Go on."

"Did you and Redpath have a row recently?"

Leila felt an inexplicable breath of coolness. "We had a slight argument this morning. Nothing much."

"Care to tell me what it was about?"

"No."

"I see." Pardey nodded as though she had given him comprehensive details. "It doesn't affect the charges against him, anyway."

"What charges?"

"Illegal entry, for a start."

Leila shook her head. "I showed John where I keep the spare key—he's free to come and go here as he pleases—and there's bound to be some simple explanation for this." Before Pardey could protest, she plucked the carving knife from the cushion and carried it to the kitchen sink. She turned on the hot water and began sponging the handle and blade.

"Hey," Pardey said gently, appearing at her side. "I'm on your side, remember?"

"Against John?"

Pardey sighed and moved towards the hall. "I'll let myself out by the tradesman's entrance."

"I'm sorry, Frank." She caught his arm. "And I'm grateful to you for coming over like this, really I am. Perhaps I'm more upset than I realised. It's just that I know John better than most people and . . ."

Pardey raised one eyebrow. "It's like that, is it?"

"Of course not." Leila was slightly taken aback at the implication that John Redpath had a special relationship with her.

"I wouldn't want *any* of my friends to think I'd set the law on them."

"Well, you haven't, so don't worry about that side of it, but please do me a favour—stop keeping that extra key outside your door. Okay?"

"It's a promise." She smiled at Pardey and was particularly careful to keep the conversation on safe ground for the remainder of his short visit. He stayed for a cup of coffee and indulged in some social chitchat, several times addressing her as his *Rostkartoffel* or *pomme frite*—standard Pardey mock-endearments—which showed that he too wanted to keep everything light and airy. But after he had gone she began to wonder if he had been overly concerned with putting her mind at rest. In lying about John's right of access to the flat she had spoken instinctively, prompted as much as anything else by a middle-class desire to avoid the sort of unpleasantness which attracted attention—but what if she did not know John Redpath nearly as well as she thought? What was it he had said to her that morning?

Something's happening to me.

What did that mean? Surely John Redpath, of all people, was too normal and too commonplace—Freudian psychology and Manichaean philosophy notwithstanding—ever to figure in one of those darkly psychotic episodes reeking of mindless savagery and sadism which were reported from time to time in the media and which she could never bring herself to study in detail. It was an axiom of everyday life that the ordinary people one knew continued to be exactly that, ordinary people, never rising very far or sinking very far, never doing anything very good or very bad.

Leila considered the proposition for a moment, deriving all the comfort she could from it, then switched on the radio and checked that the door to her apartment was securely locked.

CHAPTER 5

REDPATH AWOKE TO the sound of women's voices murmuring nearby and to the sight of a pink plastic lampshade casting its glow on a slightly uneven ceiling. He raised himself in the bed and knew at once that he was in his room in the house in Raby Street. The brown-ruled oilcloth on the floor and the assortment of shabby furniture looked familiar and reassuring, if not homely. Betty York and the gaunt, grey-cardiganed figure of Miss Connie were seated on kitchen chairs across the room, and both were looking at him with expressions of mingled interest and concern. The air in the room was cool, the day's heat having been sucked out of it by the surrounding shell of antique brickwork and plaster. It was a coolness he knew well—cheap boarding house coolness.

"Are you feeling better now, love?" Betty was dressed as when he had first met her in the park, except that she had left off the blue velvet jacket. "You gave us a bit of a fright, you know."

"I'm all right now," Redpath said, falling back on the pillow. The pear-shaped switch of the jury-rigged reading light dangled on the end of its flex a few inches above his forehead. He stared at it, freed from one reality and reluctant for the time being to commit himself to another.

This, the fact that I'm lying here in this bed, means that it was all a nightmare—the Class One to end all Class Ones. So vivid, so real, but only a bad dream. That stuff about going down into the cellar in this house and finding a monster—all a bad dream. That stuff about being in the States—all a bad dream. That stuff about finding the bodies in the bath—all a bad dream. What else could it be?

But why don't I feel happy? Why don't I feel relieved, overjoyed at being back in the real world?

72

BECAUSE OF WHAT I DID TO LEILA, THAT'S WHY.
OH GOD, WHEN I THINK OF WHAT I DID TO LEILA!

Redpath brought his left hand up into his field of view and looked at the still-weeping cut across the ball of the thumb, the cut which helped him mark the boundary between nightmare and reality. The wound had been inflicted by a real weapon, not a phantom object like Macbeth's dagger of the mind, and he could remember only too clearly those other wounds, the red-beaded lacerations which had transformed a young woman into an obscene doll. Neither sleeping nor waking was ever going to purge him of that particular memory and make him human again. Not ever. Not in an eternity of eternities . . .

"Are you sure you're all right?" Betty said, her full-lipped face drifting into view above him. "Can I get you a drink? Something like that?"

Redpath looked away from her. "I don't need anything."

"You've been having bad dreams, love."

"Really?" *Tell me something I don't know.*

"You were talking in your sleep something awful."

Redpath felt a dull stirring of interest. "What did I say?"

"Oh, I couldn't make it out." Betty glanced at Miss Connie as though seeking corroboration. "Something about being lost, I think. You were feverish, too. We nearly sent for the doctor."

But you didn't. What's the matter? Are there no shady doctors available? Are John Carradine and Walter Huston and Elisha Cooke Jr tied up somewhere?

". . . had us worried for a while, I can tell you," Betty was saying. "Have you had turns like that before, love?"

"I don't know what sort of turn I had." Redpath wondered if they had noticed his Medic-Alert bracelet. Surreptitiously, not sure of why he was doing it, he found the bracelet with his fingertips and pushed it further up his shirtsleeve, only then realising that somebody had removed his brown suede jacket while he was unconscious.

"The main thing is you're feeling better now," Betty said, smiling. "What you need is a nice cup of tea and something to eat. Come downstairs and have a bite of supper with us."

Redpath started to shake his head, then made the quite surprising discovery that he really was hungry. His stomach, it seemed, was a totally insensitive organ which demanded its customary fare regardless of the shocks and traumas experienced by other parts of his system. The idea of strong, hot tea was particularly attractive. He struggled into an upright position again, a vantage point from which he was immediately aware that his trousers were stained and crumpled, fit only for the rubbish bin. Betty's gaze followed his.

"I had an . . . accident," Redpath explained, embarrassed.

"It could happen to a bishop, love," she said unconcernedly.

"I can't go downstairs like this."

"Of course not. Don't worry about it—what size do you take?"

"What?"

Betty's plum-coloured lips twitched into an indulgent smile. "What's your waist and inside leg measurement?"

"Thirty-two and thirty-two," Redpath said, wondering if he could have strayed into yet another dream in which realities were more insidiously distorted, "but you can't . . ."

"Miss Connie will fix you up." Betty glanced at Miss Connie, who nodded almost imperceptibly, stood up and left the room without speaking. Once again he was struck by a subtle wrongness about the old woman, and this time was able to narrow it down to the fact that in spite of her stooped and frail appearance she moved with the lithe swiftness of a dancer. It was an attribute which he found oddly disconcerting.

"I expect you'd like a bath as well," Betty said, moving towards the bedroom door.

Redpath got a momentary vision of two flayed, blackened bodies in a porcelain cradle. "I don't want to put you to too much . . ."

"I'll run the water and leave out some things. Come down when you're ready, love." Betty went out and closed the door.

Redpath listened intently and heard the sound of her descending footfalls, followed a minute later by a clank of plumbing and a muted rush of water. He rolled sideways on the bed and got to his feet, wincing at the pain which flared in his groin. The room looked cheerless and more shabby than ever in the meagre radiance from the central light. He went to the window, parted the curtains and looked out into the darkness. The houses beyond formed a high, black wall, notched in one place, and through the

74

gap he could see the lights of Calbridge, glittering in a phosphorescent haze, looking as remote in time and space as the background in a da Vinci painting.

Gripped by an immense sadness, Redpath closed the curtains over and made his way through the room and out to the house's upper landing. All was now quiet in the brown dimness below. He went down the stairs and correctly identified the bathroom door as the first on the left in the short middle landing which ran through to the back of the house. The light had been left on for him. He went inside and secured the door with a small and badly aligned brass bolt. The water in the tub looked slightly yellowish, but it was hot and plentiful and some clean clothing had been placed on a cane chair.

Redpath picked up the trousers and found they were a brand-new pair of tan-coloured whipcords, with a Marks & Spencer sales label still stapled to the waist band. Rubber-stamped figures on the label informed him that the garment was of the exact size he had specified. Also on the chair were a sports shirt, underpants and socks, all with their retailer's paper tags, all crisply new.

How the . . ? He stared at the clothing in bafflement. *That room of Miss Connie's must be like the quartermaster's store!*

Moving mechanically, trying to fight off a renewed sense of unreality, Redpath took a bath and donned the fresh clothing. He rolled his discards into a bundle, took them up to his room and, after some hesitation, went back down through the house to the ground floor. A thin line of light was showing under the door of the front room. He went towards it, but before he could touch the handle the door was thrown open and he was confronted by the stubby, flashy-suited figure of Wilbur Tennent.

"Come on, John, come in," Tennent said expansively. "Don't stand on ceremony—you're one of the family now."

"Thanks," Redpath mumbled, advancing into the room. A gas fire had been lit in the hearth and sitting around it were Betty York; Miss Connie, who was knitting; and—still wearing his brown boiler suit—the ill-proportioned figure of Albert, who was nursing a teacup in his massive hands. A trolley bearing plates of sandwiches and cakes was positioned in the centre of the group. Redpath noticed that everybody in the room was smiling at him and a new kind of fear began to stir at the heart of his being, like the coiling of a worm.

This is nearly as bad as the nightmares. They think I'm like them—but that can't be true. Can it? CAN IT?

"Before you sit down, old son—take this," Tennent said, pushing a small wad of paper into Redpath's hand.

"What?" Redpath looked down and saw that he was holding a slim sheaf of banknotes. "I don't . . ."

" First day's winnings, old son—I told you Swordsmith would walk it." Tennent gripped Redpath's upper arms and gave him a playful shake. "I *told* you you wouldn't go wrong as long as you trusted me, and this is just for starters. For tomorrow I've got my eye on a filly called Parsnip Bridge which is guaranteed to . . ."

"Leave him alone," Betty York ordered sharply. "He hasn't been well."

"I was only trying to . . ."

"He isn't interested in horses. Come and sit down here, love." Betty patted the seat of the vacant easy chair next to hers. Breaking away from Tennent with a murmured apology, Redpath sat down as instructed and allowed himself to be served with tea and thick sandwiches, and all the while the coiling and uncoiling was going on inside him, restlessly, unceasingly. The worm was growing.

"Isn't this nice?" Miss Connie said in a prim, scratchy voice, speaking for the first time in Redpath's presence.

"Very nice," Albert and Betty York said in unison.

"Very nice, indeed." Miss Connie nodded and began to knit faster, signalling contentment. Redpath's gaze was drawn to the work she was producing and he saw that what he had taken to be a grey scarf had rather uneven edges, as though no attention was being paid to maintaining a constant number of stitches. It also seemed to be of inordinate length, stretching down from her chair and into a dimly-seen heap in the shadowed corner behind her. Miss Connie intercepted his gaze and smiled at him with antique dentures. He looked away from her.

Perhaps she doesn't knit anything in particular. There's something you've forgotten to do. Perhaps she just knits. For the sake of knitting.

76

Redpath concentrated for a time on his tea and the sandwiches of canned pork loaf, suddenly aware of the fact that he had not eaten since breakfast. The uneasy feeling that he had forgotten something important persisted beneath all his other misgivings for several minutes until his thoughts were distracted by the smell of cigarette smoke. There was an aromatic tang to it which suggested that the cigarette was either French or American. Redpath glanced across the semicircle and saw that Albert, now finished with his tea, was smoking and that a pack of Lucky Strikes was projecting from a pocket of his overalls. There was one place in downtown Calbridge, Redpath knew, where it was possible to buy American tobacco and cigarettes, but he had an idea they were very expensive. Certainly they were an unusual choice for a man like Albert, who gave the impression of being a typical Four Towns artisan, born and bred.

I must have noticed him with the American cigarettes earlier, Redpath mused, *and my subconscious must have locked on to that odd little detail. That's why I put Albert into the dream about being in the American town. That's the crazy way these things get built up in your mind.*

Minutes went by and there was silence in the room except for the click of Miss Connie's needles and the occasional popping and fretting of the gas fire. The drawn curtains breathed steadily in the bay window. Redpath, trapped like a fly in amber, found his mind ricocheting from one level of dread and despair to another. The knowledge that he had taken a human life, Leila's life, was ever-present behind his eyes, pounding and heaving, a loathsome cancer which could never be excised. At times the focus of his thoughts would drift away from it and other things would become briefly prominent—red-oozing deathmasks, organic slurries advancing on glowing green tiles, blackened bodies like choice Pompeian obscenities, cellars whose walls reached out with yearning tentacles, nightmares all—and at those times he would try to escape, and in fleeing would run headlong into the most terrible spectre of the lot, that of Leila with her eyes turning into glass buttons, and the awful wheel would begin to grind again. The tumult of guilt and horror was emotionally exhausting, and in spite of the fact that he had been unconscious throughout the latter part of the day Redpath found himself wishing for sleep, even with the risk of further dreams. Yielding to the fuggy warmth of the room, he closed his eyes for a moment and when he opened them Wilbur Tennent had leaned forward in his chair and was pointing at him in gleeful accusation.

"Keeeeeeee . . ." Tennent intoned in a high-pitched whine, his eyes intent on Redpath's, ". . . eeee pright on to the end of the road, kee . . . pright on to the end."

Redpath stared back at him, transfixed.

"That's a good idea," Betty said, beginning to sing. "Though the way be long, let your heart beat strong, keep right on round the . . . Why aren't you singing, love?" She gave Redpath an inquisitive nudge.

"I . . ." He looked from her to Miss Connie and Albert, both of whom were chanting almost inaudibly in time with Tennent, their faces wearing expressions of intemperate happiness. "I can't sing."

"You needn't be shy in front of us—you're a member of the family now," Tennent said. "We often have a good old singsong at nights instead of watching that rubbish they put on the TV. Come on, John!" He gestured like a choir-master, his hands almost touching Redpath's face. "Though the way be weary, still journey on, till you come to your hap . . . peeabode . . ."

I'm not a member of your bloody family, Redpath thought, but his lips had already begun to move in response to Tennent's coaxing and he listened with acute embarrassment to his own voice following the words of the old song. *This can't be happening to me. What have I forgotten to do? Please let me go to bed.*

He made up his mind to get to his feet and excuse himself from the company as politely as possible when the song had ended, but when the moment came he found himself in the grip of the same kind of paralysis he had known as a gauche child and which had held him prisoner through innumerable church services and school concerts. All he had to do was stand up, utter a meaningless pleasantry and go to bed—and yet that simple course of action was quite beyond him. The others in the group were exerting a psychic pressure which rendered him helpless, and if they wanted to sit around and sing until dawn he would have no recourse but to remain with them. Redpath looked at the clock on the mantelpiece, saw that it was more than an hour

78

until midnight, and a groan almost escaped his lips as the company finished the first song and immediately merged it into the beginning of *Lily Of Laguna* with practised fluency.

Their voices were hushed, almost reverent, dominated by the incongruously musical tones of Albert, who smoked incessantly and grinned his acromegalic grin as song followed song. Miss Connie industriously added to the formless mass of grey wool in the corner behind her chair. Betty York smiled warmly and encouragingly at Redpath each time she caught his eye. Wilbur Tennent sat bolt upright and occasionally conducted the performance, gold cuff-links glistering, his neat, chubby, handsome features suffused with bonhomie. Redpath thought of alcoholics working desperately to convince themselves that they were glad to be sitting in a rented meeting room drinking cocoa, and his sense of suffocation increased. A crane-fly alighted on the wall opposite to him and began to vibrate in a steady and mindless palsy, minute after minute after minute, like a tiny machine which had developed some unbalancing and irremediable fault . . .

"Tomorrow's another day, folks," Betty announced abruptly when the hands of the clock stood at a quarter to twelve. "And I need my beauty sleep."

She stood up, absent-mindedly smoothing her Liz Taylor torso with both hands in a manner which reminded Redpath that, incredibly, in the beginning he had thought of her as the partner for a sleazy sexual adventure. That beginning had been earlier in the same day, little more than twelve hours into the past, but he had come a long way since then. He got to his feet and turned towards the door, cautiously keeping his distance from Betty in case, through some gross misjudgement on her part, she tried to reintroduce the element of sexuality into their relationship. Wilbur Tennent had stood up also and now he was smiling at Redpath and frowning at the same time in an expression of rueful perplexity.

"John, old son," he said, "you wouldn't run out on us, would you?"

Redpath floundered for a moment, lost for a response. "Of course not. I mean . . ."

"Good boy, John. And don't forget about Parsnip Bridge."

"Good night," Redpath said, addressing himself to the entire group, and in a few seconds he was ascending through the tall, narrow house with wraith-like speed and silence, taking the stairs two and three at a time. He reached the top landing, went into his room and closed the door. The pendant lamp stirred slightly, activated by his arrival, causing uneasy movements of shadows. Redpath's relief at being alone was tempered by a sudden appreciation of the fact that all the long night lay ahead of him and that he was to spend it amid an assemblage of furniture which looked inhospitable and accidental, like items gathered in a shabby saleroom. It was highly unlikely that he would be able to sleep in such surroundings, tired though he was. He hesitated near the door, rubbing his arms to subdue the goose-pimples which had been brought out by the unheated air, then crossed to the bed and got underneath the quilt without undressing.

After a couple of minutes he began to feel warm again, but that served only to make the house seem colder and more hostile by comparison. His body-heated tent was a solitary outpost, menaced on all sides by watchful and implacable enemies.

Enemies? Don't be stupid. Don't fight it. You're safe here. You're one of the family now . . .

He listened to the sounds of the house bedding down for the night, the various distant rushings of water, the thrumming of pipes, the muted closing of doors. Somebody padded quietly past the door of his own room and he guessed it was Wilbur Tennent making for his quarters at the front of the house. In the silence which followed he became aware that the ceiling light was making a faint muttering sound, indicative of a poor electrical connection. He considered getting out of bed and turning it off, but taking the plunge into sudden darkness seemed a bold and extreme course of action, one which should be postponed until he had had time to get the lie of the land, to weigh all the consequences. He pulled the quilt more tightly around himself, slipped down into a more comfortable position and—purely as an experiment—closed his eyes to gauge the possibility of his eventually being able to sleep . . .

The nightmare was immediately identifiable as a nightmare, and that made it a Class Two. Gratitude flickered in an isolated fragment of his consciousness, but only briefly. Knowledge that

80

a dream *was* a dream was supposed to dilute the effect, to enable him to stand back and take an indulgent interest in the latest playlet being offered by his subconscious, but on this occasion something seemed to be going wrong. Once again he was standing on a stair and looking down on a broad expanse of green-and-cream checker-board—the hall floor of the psychophysiology building at the Jeavons Institute—and he knew the floor was not really there, because he had quit the programme and would never be returning to it, and yet the image was impinging on his senses with a sharp, uncompromising clarity which proclaimed that it was part of the external material world.

What is this? Am I capable of double-double-think?

Redpath watched in taut fascination as the floor tiles began to exhibit colour changes, some of them becoming blue and semi-transparent while others metamorphosed into squares of amber, ruby and citrine. They seemed to be illuminated from under-neath by lights which continually varied in intensity, creating patterns with shifting emphases, and again there was a sense of movement as though each square capped a cell containing a small, nervous animal. The vision held no significance for Red-path—compared to some of his recent imaginings it was almost beautiful—and yet as he scanned the warm-glowing geometries he was gripped by a sense of apprehension which left him sick and paralysed. There was an imminence, a quickening dread, a bleak certainty that none of the terrors which had gone before could even begin to prepare him for what was coming next.

I was lucky last time—this nightmare never really got started. But it has started now.

There was a stirring at the edge of his vision, a stealthy advancement, and he became aware of a creeping brown tide. It resembled old thready blood, bulked up to the consistency of sludge with millions of writhing slug-like strips of liver. The leading edge of the tide wavered and hesitated and rippled as it crossed the patterned floor, extending slim and tremulous pseudo-pods on to new squares, sometimes withdrawing them at once as though conditions had been judged unfavourable, more often gorging and swelling them with dark fluids until yet another section of the checker-board had been submerged by the loath-some organic slurry. Redpath, trapped in the chilly immobility

81

of the dreamer, willed himself to do something, anything which would break the paralysis and let him make it clear to the universe at large that he wanted no part of what was happening, that he was not some death-oriented creature willingly going forward to . . . *what?*

The beginnings of a retching moan shaped themselves low in his body, then came the incredible realisation that this—the slow engulfment by a slurry of sentient blood clots—was not the ultimate horror he had been anticipating. There was something else to come. Something much worse.

His gaze was drawn to an area at the middle of the floor where four tiles made up a larger square which until that moment had not changed from their original coloration. As he watched, the larger square grew darker and darker until quite suddenly it resembled a transparent hatch leading down into a well of utter blackness. A pinpoint of light was born in the centre of the jetty rectangle. It grew brighter, then split in two, finally resolving itself into a tiny blue-white disc accompanied by a white star-like speck of brilliance.

For one instant a weight seemed to lift from Redpath's soul. *It's just like looking through an astronomical telescope,* he thought. *Why, for God's sake, that could almost be the Earth and the . . .*

Abruptly, without warning, the flimsy word-edifice of his rationalization was swept away in a torrent of primitive emotion. Fear mingled and spumed with hatred and disgust and anger, but always the fear was predominant, always fear was the under-lying matrix, the cataract which carried all else rushing onwards and downwards in its dark bores and fluxes, fear, fear, fear . . .

NO! The voice threatened to explode Redpath's skull. *NO! NO! NO!*

He awoke shivering in the coldness of the bedroom, and for a moment almost smiled as he took in its commonplace ambience of pink plastic lampshades and flowered wallpaper. The great thing about nightmares was how one felt on wakening up. This was the real world, a world which might look tired and shabby, but which at least had the advantage that as long as one remained securely locked into it nothing very far out of the ordinary would ever . . .

Leila!

Redpath's eyes widened and he groaned aloud as he recalled the true extent of the nightmare his life had become, a nightmare from which there were to be no respites, waking or sleeping. He threw back the quilt, got out of bed and went to a tallboy which supported a speckled circular mirror. Resting his forearms on the varnished wood, he stooped forward until he could see himself in the glass. The startling thing about the face which regarded him from the left-handed universe within the mirror was that it was immediately identifiable as his own face, the one John Redpath had always possessed. True, it was paler than usual, so that the freckles were more clearly visible, and the close-waved brown hair was less orderly, but the eyes in particular were those of a sane man. It hardly seemed possible, and in his state of mind it also seemed vaguely unfair after what he had been through—as though he had been denied some hard-earned mark of distinction. Staring solemnly at the uninvolved, unscathed bystander in the glass, Redpath felt a compulsion to speak, to test the synchrony of both pairs of lips. The rules against such abnormal behaviour seemed to have been suspended. There was a humming in his ears, as of a distant generator.

"I told you," he whispered accusingly, taking the part of his alter ego, "there was something you forgot to do."

"What? What did I forget?"

"Look closely at me. Can't you see it yet?"

For a moment Redpath was at a loss, then he became aware that his mood and perceptions had undergone a change. He felt a quasi-religious exultation. The air about him appeared to vibrate and sparkle.

"No," he said urgently. "Not that!"

He straightened up and tried to turn away from the mirror as it dawned on him that the catalogue of the day's disasters was not yet complete, that in the onrush of dream and drama he had been tricked into forgetting to take his customary dose of Epanutin. His brown suede zipper-up was draped over the back of a chair and, if memory could still be trusted, his emergency supply of phenobarbitone capsules was in one of the pockets. He took one step towards the chair, knowing as he did so that the action was entirely futile, then the electrical storms of an

83

epileptic seizure swept through his brain, erasing, cleansing, relieving him of all the onerous burdens and responsibilities of consciousness.

The darkness which flowed around him was both heavy and sweet.

The miracle was a small one—but significant.

The miracle was so small as to be indetectable to anyone else—but its effects were profound, and Redpath was deeply grateful for them.

He awoke to the clean, pewter-coloured light of sanity, knowing who he was, what he was, and what he had to do about it, and the feeling was deeply comforting.

At first he was aware of nothing but a pale grey rectangle, a trapezium of pearly radiance, and for a second he feared it was an extension of his most recent nightmare, then came mental and physical orientation. He was lying on the floor of his room in the house in Raby Street and he could see the coming of dawn beyond the single window. The real world, he knew, was out there waiting for him, and there was nothing to prevent his rejoining it. Its demands might be great, but he was equal to them. He knew himself to be capable of paying his dues in order to regain that most prized of possessions—his peace of mind.

Redpath moved his arms and legs experimentally, in preparation for standing up. There was some stiffness in the muscles but no noticeable degree of pain, meaning that he had experienced only a *petit mal* which had quickly given way to normal sleep. That was something else for which he could feel grateful. He gripped the end of the bed and pulled himself up to a standing position. The central lamp was still emitting its pink glow, and in the conflict of natural and artificial lights the over-furnished room looked aggressively squalid, like a set design for a play in the *Love On The Dole* genre.

Redpath placed the back of a hand on his brow and surveyed the room bemusedly, trying to assess the extent of the madness which must have gripped him on the previous day. The entire period seemed remote and shadowy—even the dreadful episode resulting in Leila's death—and the only explanation which came to mind was that he had experienced a drastic side-effect of

Compound 183. That was something the police would have to take into consideration when they looked into his story, and Henry Nevison would have to give corroboratory evidence, even if it spelt out the end of one of his most cherished research projects.

The thought of seeing the police and having his crime recorded and categorised, reduced to the compass of typed A4 sheets in a buff file, suffused Redpath with a longing to get clear of the house and its odd set of inhabitants. He glanced at his watch, saw that the time was 5.33 and tried winding the watch without removing it from his wrist. His fingers kept slipping off the tiny knurled projection and it suddenly came to him that he was deathly cold. He took his suede jacket from the chair, slipped into it and pulled the zip up to his throat, trapping his body's heat. The sound of the brass teeth meshing together was unnaturally loud.

That's it, young feller my lad, he thought. *You're free to go. Really?*

In spite of his newly-regained and blessed rationality, Redpath found himself entertaining a suspicion that it was all too straightforward and easy, that he would not simply be able to stroll away and merge safely into the mainstreams of life. The house and its denizens seemed to have a composite personality, and his instincts told him that personality was to some extent deranged, and furthermore that it would be reluctant to let him go free. It might be better to delay his escape bid until there was traffic in the street outside. Surely he would be safer if there were people nearby whose attention he could attract.

Get a grip, man! What are you playing at?

Cursing himself for having yielded to cinema-induced childish fantasies, Redpath went to the bedroom door and opened it. The landing outside was dark and empty.

Of course it's empty! Who did you expect? Bela Lugosi? Or that kid, Linda Blair from The Exorcist, with her head turned backwards and a nightdress covered with green vomit?

I told you—get a GRIP!

Moving with a curious timidity, Redpath went out onto the landing and paused to listen to the house. There was a faint sound of snoring from the direction of the front room, indicating

85

that Wilbur Tennent was in there and still fast asleep. Reassured by the touch of normality, Redpath walked quietly to the stairs and proceeded down it to the next landing. The door to the master bedroom, the one he believed to be occupied by Betty York, was very slightly ajar and he passed it on tiptoe, fearful of disturbing her. Next on the left was Miss Connie's door, then he went down three steps to the rear landing where he could see all the way through to the back of the house.

The window at the end was shining with dawn light, and the yellow fleur-de-lis hung motionless at its centre like a watchful bird. Redpath jerked his head back as the pungent odour of cloves wafted into his nostrils and almost as quickly faded away. *It was never really there,* he thought. *Spook smells. Synaesthesia.*

He averted his eyes from the partly open door of the bathroom, which was only two paces away from him, and slowly went down the remaining stair to the ground floor. All that was left for him to do now was to go to the double set of front doors, let himself out through them—provided they were not fitted with burglar-proof locks which required a key to operate them from the inside—and walk off through the quiet morning streets in the direction of the Woodstock Road. He was practically free and clear! The notion that he might have to spend some time fumbling with locks, time in which somebody could approach him from behind, prompted Redpath to turn and look back towards the kitchen. Its door was wide open, and in the grey dimness beyond something white stirred feebly in mid-air like a giant moth.

Redpath's hand flew to his mouth and the white object reacted simultaneously, jolting him into the realization that he was looking at the reflection of his own face in a kitchen mirror. He stood his ground, aware that to run at that precise instant would be to make some kind of dreadful admission. In the pounding seconds which followed he moved slowly to one side, conducting an experiment, and his reflection slid out of sight as the laws of optics demanded, proving that the mirror really was a mirror and that the friendly old rules of physics still held sway. The new angle of reflection brought into view a patch of crimson which he immediately identified as being the cellar door located in the nearer corner of the kitchen. He nodded in satisfaction, turned to walk to the front door, then halted in mid-stride, frowning.

What's going on here? I never actually saw a bright red cellar door in the kitchen—that was a bit from that bloody awful nightmare about walking down into the house's stomach!

Redpath stood perfectly still, stroking the day's growth of bristles on his chin, working out an explanation. The obvious one, the one the experts always used to discredit people who claimed to have precognitive dreams, was that he *had* glimpsed the red door without being consciously aware of it. That was a good explanation. It was a neat, sensible bit of reasoning—but the main trouble was that he could not bring himself to accept it. He was quite positive that on the few occasions on which he had traversed the hall the door to the kitchen had been fully closed, and that it would have been impossible for him to see anything inside.

All right, then—if one explanation failed to fit another one would take its place. Why, he wondered, should he bother about an explanation, anyway? Why not be content to get out while the going was good?

He teetered on the balls of his feet, knowing perfectly well why he needed to hound down and eradicate every last scrap of mystery concerning the events of the past night and day. The house had made him afraid. It had mounted an attack on the citadel of his materialism and commonsense, and if he flew now— half-convinced of the existence of supernatural terrors—the house would have won. It would have turned him into a different person, and he would never again be able to face the dark without reacting like a scared child or a superstitious savage. And life was hard enough as it was ...

Redpath turned back and walked to the kitchen door.

The room was long and half-way down the left-hand wall was a cracked porcelain sink which was stacked high with unwashed dishes. That, too, was exactly as he had visualized it in the dream, but it failed to disturb him because it could be written off as deduction from experience. Older houses of this type were remarkably similar in their layout; the obvious lack of modernisation indicated that an old type of sink would still be in place; and Betty York had not struck him as the sort of person who would scrupulously wash up after every meal. There was also a refrigerator standing in the predicted corner, but it was in one of the few logical positions for such an item of equipment. The cellar door, presuming it did actually lead down into a cellar, was going to be the test case.

Redpath advanced two steps into the room and looked to his right, into the corner which had been screened from his view by the kitchen door. There was another door there, one which was painted an incongruous fire-engine red. A floating, dream-like sensation enveloped him as he reached out with his right hand and grasped the door's old-fashioned farmhouse-style latch.

Hey, doc—there's no need to go ahead with this! I've just thought of the perfect explanation. It's our old friend Compound 183 again! You picked up details of the kitchen layout by telepathy from Betty York or the others. It's the sort of thing that's been happening to you all the time lately. Can't you see that?

Redpath opened the door and was barely able to discern the beginning of a flight of stone steps which led downwards into darkness. The air which wafted up around him was warmer than he had expected. Warm and heavy. He moved forward, went down two steps to the limit of his vision and paused, listening.

Oh boy, I can't believe you're really doing this. You know what it's like, don't you? It's like that big scene in all the old horror flicks, the one where the hero is dumb enough to walk right into the monster's den. Every kid in the stalls is under the seat screaming for him to turn back, but he keeps right on going. Honest to God, John, I thought you'd more sense . . .

Redpath went down a third step and paused again, straining to penetrate the darkness with his senses. Something below him made a wet sound, a sucking sound.

Slughhh. Slughhh. Slughhh.

He withdrew to the second step, shaking his head, trying to make a connection in his memory between the sound and the various pieces of obsolete and noisy plumbing that an old house might contain.

Slughhh. Slughhh. Slughhh.

"All right, house—you win," Redpath whispered, retreating to the top of the cellar steps. He closed the red door and, no longer caring about the possibility of being heard by anyone in the upper part of the building, strode quickly through the hall to the inner entrance door and unlocked it. The solid door was secured by two shoot-bolts as well as by a Yale lock, but Redpath undid all three fastenings with a nervous urgency which would not be denied.

A few seconds later he was outside in the quiet, morning-grey streets, outside and running.

PART TWO

Interlude

CHAPTER 6

WATCHING THE TOWN'S diurnal return to life did something to
restore Redpath's faith in the ubiquity of the commonplace, but
it was a bitter-sweet experience. A barrier had dropped solidly
into place between him and all the other citizens of the Four
Towns. He felt like a stranger, someone with an artificial reason
for being there, like a visiting reporter trying to get the feel of
the place for a television feature. During the hours he spent
walking in the town centre or sipping coffee in steamy glass-
fronted caverns, he looked at the faces of perhaps a thousand
people and he knew that not one of those people had ever slain
a fellow human being, or had any trouble distinguishing between
fantasy and reality, or had allowed himself to believe that a
shabby old house could develop a malevolent personality of its
own. He was totally alone, cut off.

When he felt he was ready to face the police he glanced at his
watch, saw that the time was exactly nine o'clock and wondered
briefly if his subconscious had chosen to wait for the beginning
of what might be normal business hours for the CID. It was, he
thought, the sort of lame-brained thing a subconscious like his
might do. He set down a half-finished mug of weak coffee, went
out into Calbridge's shopping and commercial area, and walked
the best part of a mile to the police station. It was a compact
two-storey building of blue-red brick, with a gateway at one side
leading into an enclosed yard used for parking official vehicles.

He was going up the entrance steps when a grey saloon car
which had been turning into the yard stopped so abruptly in the
gateway that its suspension creaked. The driver's window slid
down to reveal a fair-skinned, strongly-built man whose face
looked familiar to Redpath. *Pardey*, he thought. *Frank Pardey.
How did I know that?*

93

"You," Pardey said coldly, aiming his forefinger like a pistol. "Over here!"

Surprised to find that he was still capable of indignation, Redpath paused long enough to show that he was unused to peremptory commands, then walked slowly to the car. "Yes?"

"John Redpath, isn't it?"

"Yes." *I remember now—we met at a party somewhere. Probably Vicki Simpson's place.*

"What are you doing here, Redpath? What do you want?"

Perplexed by the other man's hostility, Redpath decided to jolt him in the hardest possible way. "You know Leila Mostyn?"

"What of it?"

"I . . . I stabbed her to death yesterday."

Pardey studied Redpath with blue eyes which showed neither shock nor surprise, only a considered and calm dislike. "Do yourself a favour, Redpath," he snapped. "Bugger off."

"What?"

"You heard me—bug off."

"You don't believe me?" Redpath said, angered by Pardey's refusal to react in an appropriate manner. "All right, I'll talk to somebody at the desk." He turned to walk back to the police station entrance.

"Just a minute," Pardey said impatiently. "Is this some kind of a sick joke?"

"Joke?" Redpath gave a shaky laugh. "That's a good one. Joke!"

Pardey's eyes narrowed in speculation. "This thing about Leila—when did it happen?"

"Yesterday lunchtime, in her flat. About one."

"You're sure of that?"

"It's not the sort of thing I'd be hazy about."

"Well, I talked to Leila yesterday around six o'clock and there was nothing the matter with her," Pardey said in a matter-of-fact voice, his eyes intent on Redpath's. "What do you say to that?"

Redpath's mouth went dry and he felt a painful, chilly prickling on his forehead and cheeks. "But I . . ."

"I'll tell you what you did yesterday lunchtime—you went round to Leila's flat when she wasn't there and you cut up one of her cushions with a kitchen knife. The only person you hurt was yourself."

Redpath gave the detective a numb smile before turning away to grasp the metal bars of the nearby gate. He stood that way for a moment, bracing himself against the convulsions in his stomach, then brought up the coffee he had drunk a few minutes earlier. The silt-coloured fluid spattered noisily on the concrete.

"Get into the car," he heard Pardey saying in the distance. There was a sensation of being manhandled, the smell of orange peel and cigarette ash from the car's interior, rotating street images as the vehicle was backed up a short distance and was driven away from the police station. A bus momentarily filled the view ahead—a meaningless assembly of saffron-coloured sheet metal and posters—and slid away to one side as Pardey overtook it.

"I'm lost," Redpath mumbled. "Everything . . . *melts.*"

Pardey glanced sideways at him. "What is it, Redpath? Drugs?"

"I think so."

"You *think* so?"

Redpath brought all his attention to bear on the task of arranging words in a logical sequence. "I work at the Jeavons Institute. They've been trying some stuff out on me—doing tests. I think something has gone wrong. Look, I've got to see Leila for myself."

"She works at the Jeavons too, doesn't she?"

"I believe so, but then what I believe isn't necessarily . . ."

"Would she be there by this time? It's almost half nine."

"She should be there," Redpath said, trying to rid himself of a vision of a slim, tapering back hideously disfigured by stab wounds. "I'd like to see her."

Pardey nodded ungraciously. "Just remember—no funny stuff. If Leila wasn't a friend of mine you'd be facing charges right now. In fact, if you don't get some pretty solid backing for what you've just told me . . ." He glanced at Redpath again, compressed his lips and returned to the business of driving with the air of a man whose natural instincts were being sorely thwarted.

Recognising the advisability of remaining silent, Redpath

closed his eyes and rode with the motions of the car, swallowing repeatedly in an attempt to cleanse the sour taste of bile from his mouth and throat.

For months after the death of his father Redpath had been tormented by dreams in which his father was still alive. He had always awakened from them saddened and disturbed, with his grief renewed, but while the illusions still held good for him he had known moments of utter happiness in which he had looked on his living father with joy, appreciation and contentment, understanding that to do otherwise where a loved one was concerned was to squander life itself.

The same kind of emotion gripped him now as he watched Leila Mostyn across the small conference table in Nevison's office. She was miraculously and beautifully alive, unharmed, untouched, dressed exactly as he would have pictured her in a white lab coat, filmy blouse and tweed skirt. He no longer quite trusted the evidence of his senses, but it seemed to him as he told his story that she was genuinely troubled on his behalf, that without realising what was happening she had come close to entering that special, binding, exclusive relationship for which he yearned and for which he would be prepared to face the events of the previous twenty-four hours all over again.

In his account of those events Redpath, as requested by Nevison, paid as much attention to the imaginary as to the real, filling in every scrap of detail he could remember of hallucination, dream and nightmare. He spoke for almost an hour, during which time both Pardey and Nevison took occasional notes to supplement the tape recording which was being made. At the passages which concerned her, particularly the death scene, Leila's colouring deepened and she stared fixedly at her hands, looking both thoughtful and embarrassed. Redpath took the opportunity to apologise to her during a lull in which Nevison was changing tapes.

"Dreams ought to be private," he said. "I'll bet this sort of thing isn't in your contract."

She gave him a wan smile. "I didn't realise what you were going through."

"Didn't realise it myself." He tried to return the smile. "And do you know the worst of it? It's just struck me this minute—somebody has half-inched my bicycle!"

"How can you joke about it?"

"It's no joke," he assured her with mock-seriousness, the privilege of being able to talk to Leila again producing a sudden lift in his spirits. "There was a brand-new pump on that machine. It's probably been given a new paint job by this time and shipped over to the Continent. I hear there's a big racket in . . ."

"Tape number two," Nevison cut in. "Just carry on from where you left off, John."

Redpath nodded and continued his narrative, pausing only to clarify points raised by Nevison, and going on to an account of his mild epileptic seizure and the early-morning departure from the house in Raby Street. In retrospect, in the book-lined, wax-scented comfort of Nevison's office, he was tempted to omit details of how he had tried to investigate the cellar and had allowed himself to be panicked into headlong flight by nothing more than an unexplained noise. The presence of the tape recorder reminded him that he had set out to provide an exhaustive description of an abnormal state of mind. He gave a fair report of the incident, glancing sheepishly from one face to the other as he did so, and concluded with his abortive visit to the Calbridge police station and the meeting with Pardey. When he had finished speaking the quietness in the room was so intense that the tape machine suddenly seemed defective, whirring and scraping as it tried to record nothing. Nevison switched it off, causing some internal component to reverberate like a tuning fork.

"I'll kick off by saying I think I owe John an apology," Frank Pardey said, looking up from his notes. "I'd no idea of the sort of thing that goes on here, and I didn't know there had been any experimenting with drugs. I'm here mainly as a friend of Leila's, of course, but it seems to me that if you're going to use drugs that gives a man hallucinations you should keep a close eye on him till the stuff wears off."

Nevison shook his head. "The compounds we use aren't hallucinogens."

"They just make you see things that aren't there," Redpath said sarcastically, surprised and angered to find that Nevison was still disclaiming responsibility for what had happened to him.

"That's what telepathy *is*," Nevison replied. "Seeing things that aren't in front of your eyes."

"And that's another thing—telepathy!" Pardey shifted in his chair and gave the others a perplexed smile. "I thought I knew everything that went on around this town—but *telepathy* experiments! And at the Jeavons, of all places!"

"The idea is fairly widely accepted."

" Not around South Haverside it isn't," Pardey said emphatically. "Some people in these parts still have their doubts about the telephone."

Redpath stared at Pardey with a dull sense of wonderment, half-convinced that the detective had said something significant. Now that he thought of it, the Jeavons Institute—traditional, conventional, hidebound, less a seat of learning than a repository for technical knowledge required by local industry—seemed an unusual place to find time and money being spent on para-psychological research. Because of his own close association with the project he had never stopped to consider . . .

"The thing that really intrigues me," Nevison said firmly, dismissing what he obviously regarded as side issues, "is the management capability of the various levels of John's consciousness, the ability to take selected elements of perception and fit them into a unified pattern with extra-sensory or subjective elements." He leaned forward to peer into Redpath's face.

"John, do you fully understand that I wasn't at Leila's flat yesterday? She borrowed my car to pop home for ten minutes."

"I know that now."

"When Leila drove the car away from the house, couldn't you see her at the wheel?"

"No—the sun was shining on the side windows. It dazzled me."

"Otherwise everything looked normal?"

"Well, everything seemed to be rippling a bit. I remember I started thinking about detached retinas."

"In other words, you had a slight feeling you were watching an image projected on . . ."

"Excuse me, Doctor Nevison," Pardey interjected, "I'm the odd man here and I want to get out of your way as quickly as possible—but I need to ask John a couple of questions first."

An expression of annoyance flickered on Nevison's greyish face, but he made an ushering gesture in Redpath's direction. "I'm sure John won't mind."

"Thanks." Pardey consulted his notebook before glancing at Redpath. "This woman with the room full of goods and provisions—have you any idea what her second name is?"

"No." Redpath was suddenly aware of being back in the normal world, where different types of people had different types of preoccupation. "I only know her as Miss Connie."

"How about the man Albert?"

"Just Albert."

"I see. Have you any idea how these people support themselves?"

"None at all—I was only there for a matter of hours and the subject didn't come up. I think Albert may have been in the steelworks at one time." For the second time in a couple of minutes Redpath sensed that Pardey, with his uncompromising practicality, had managed to touch on something worth thinking about. Yesterday had been Tuesday, an ordinary working day, but nobody in the house in Raby Street had gone to work. What did they do for a living?

"It all sounds a bit . . ." Pardey scraped his pen along the spiral wire binding of his notebook, producing a noise like a miniature rattle, and his blue eyes were pensive. "Is there a telephone I could use? I want to call the station."

"Along the landing, second door on the right," Nevison told him. He waited until the detective had left the room, then gave Redpath a smile which was unexpectedly sympathetic. Redpath raised his eyebrows and turned his gaze towards the window, refusing to be won over too quickly.

"John, I don't want you to think you're on your own in this thing," Nevison said. "You've had a very unpleasant time of it, and as head of the department I feel responsible. None of us foresaw the exact manner in which Compound 183 would affect your perceptions, and . . ."

"But you said the drug had nothing to do with it," Redpath blurted. "You as good as said I was going gaga on my own."

Nevison smiled again. "What I said was that the compound

99

didn't cause you to have any hallucinations. I still insist that you are picking up telepathic emanations in visual form—they could be coming from anywhere—and that you haven't yet learned to interpret them properly."

"There's no interpreting to do—when you see something you see it."

"It's not as simple as that, John, believe me. If you take a photograph of a television set and hand it to an aboriginal tribesman who has never seen a television or even a photograph before, he'll have absolutely no idea what you've given him. All he will be able to see is a flat sheet with some coloured stains on it. Similarly, a wiring diagram for that same set could be meaningless to you, but for an electronics engineer it would be crammed with crystal-clear information. Do you see what I mean?"

"I see what you mean, but you don't mean what I mean."

"Let's move on a bit," Nevison said patiently. "In that dream you had about being in the United States—what was the name of the town?"

"Gilpinston."

"And the state?"

"I think it was Illinois." Redpath spoke reluctantly, aware that Nevison was setting up some kind of a trap.

"Right. To the best of your knowledge, have you ever heard of a place called Gilpinston, Illinois?"

"Never, but I don't see what . . ."

"I'm taking a bit of a gamble here," Nevison said, standing up and going to one of his bookshelves, "but it's all in a good cause." He took a large, weighty atlas from the shelf, opened it at the gazetteer section and placed the book in Redpath's lap. "Go ahead, John, look up Gilpinston."

Redpath did as instructed, running a finger down the narrow columns of small type. He stopped, feeling a tremor of unease, when he reached an entry in which the words "Gilpinston, Ill. U.S.A." were followed by a page number and a set of map references.

"What does this mean?" he said, frowning up at Nevison. "How did you know it would be there?"

Nevison returned to his desk and sat down before replying. "I didn't. I never heard of Gilpinston until you mentioned it this morning."

Leila left her chair and stood beside Redpath, resting her hand on his shoulder while she checked the gazetteer entry herself. "Are you putting this forward as proof that telepathy was involved?"

"It isn't as simple as that," Nevison said ruefully. "It could be telepathy or unconscious retention of a place name. What I was trying to demonstrate to John is that the relationship between his mind and his brain is more complex than he previously thought. I'll give you another example from the same dream sequence . . . John, have you ever been to the States?"

"Never." Redpath answered automatically, much more concerned with the fact that Leila had remained at his side. He could smell the light blossomy perfume she favoured.

"I thought not—and yet when you were describing trying to turn the light on in that basement you said the switch was upside down. You said you had to push the toggle up to turn the light on."

Redpath shrugged. "What of it?"

"Switches are like that in the States. Pushing them up turns them on."

"That can't be right. I mean, it's a natural movement to turn something on by bringing your hand down. I mean . . ." Redpath's voice tailed off uncertainly as he began to realise that right from the beginning he and Nevison had been arguing on two entirely different levels.

"That could be unconscious retention, as well," Leila said. "Anybody who has seen as many American films as John could have absorbed that fact without realising he was doing it."

"You're absolutely right," Nevison replied equably. "All I want is for John to appreciate that mental scenarios which are presented to him—no matter whether they are internally or externally inspired—cannot be treated like Disney cartoons. It may be that the greatest problem in telepathic communication will be incompatability between sender and receiver. We may have to anticipate a plethora of interpretation difficulties."

Leila exhaled sharply, with what sounded to Redpath like impatience. "Shouldn't you be more concerned with the clinical effects of your experimental drugs? I know this isn't my department, but John has practically lost a day out of his life, and it seems to me that almost anything could have happened to him yesterday."

"I'm arranging for him to have a full check-up this afternoon before we go back on to the routine test procedures."

Redpath gave a theatrical cough. "Just letting you two know I'm still here," he said. "Don't I get consulted about what happens next?"

"Of course, but I assumed you'd wish to press ahead with the test schedule while conditions are exceptional," Nevison said. "How do you feel at this moment?"

"All right, I suppose." Redpath took stock of mind and body, and discovered that he felt relaxed and confident, sustained by the knowledge that Leila was alive and that the nightmare had ended. "Actually, I feel pretty good right now. It's as if that turn I had during the night did something to . . ." He broke off at the sound of the door being opened.

"Sorry I took so long," Frank Pardey said, entering the room with the majorette's knee-lifting gait which looked so out of place for a man of his size and build. He dropped into the chair he had vacated and checked something in his notebook before addressing himself to Redpath.

"It turns out that our friend Tennent has some form," he said. "I'd like to talk to him."

"What has he done?"

"It looks like gambling swindles mostly—he seems to have ripped off bookmakers in four different spots up and down the country."

"Can't they afford it?" Redpath said, thinking of Tennent's jovial friendliness which was perhaps the only thing he would care to remember about the previous day. He disliked the idea of his being instrumental in the chubby gambler's arrest.

"I daresay most of them can afford it, but there's something else," Pardey said in a businesslike voice. "He's wanted for questioning in connection with the disappearance of one Reginald Adams Selvidge—otherwise known as Prince Reginald—who used to run some kind of a mind-reading act in the south coast summer theatres. Vanished about eight years ago."

102

"Mind-reading act?" Redpath glanced at the others in surprise. "That's odd."

Pardey nodded. "That's what I thought. I don't suppose you ran into *him* yesterday?"

"Why should I?"

"No reason. I was only joking."

Some joke, Redpath thought, divining what had been in the detective's mind. *I see the joke, and I see the implications. That place in Raby Street is like a rest home for freaks—and I was welcomed into it with open arms . . .*

Pardey closed his notebook, put it away in his pocket and stood up. "Okay, John, let's go and pick up your bicycle."

Redpath blinked at him. "Where is it?"

"Well, I'm hoping it's where you told us it was—at 131 Raby Street."

"I don't want to go back there so soon," Redpath said quickly.

"Why not?"

"It would be embarrassing for me. Those people thought I was moving in with them yesterday . . . ."

"It's a peculiar thing about that address," Nevison put in unexpectedly, "but it seems almost familiar to me."

"You want to get your bicycle back, don't you?" Pardey said, watching Redpath's face with amused interest.

"I can send somebody to collect it."

"I wonder," Nevison mused, "was the place ever owned by a doctor or a dentist?"

On his final word a faint but unmistakable smell of cloves stole into Redpath's nostrils, and he knew on the instant that as a small child he had been to the house in Raby Street—perhaps only once—for dental treatment. The synaesthetic aroma of the clove oil used in mouthwashes was what had swamped his senses as he had entered the hallway with Betty York.

I was there before, damn it all!

The revelation, coming like a clear shaft of sunlight, produced an immediate if not entirely rational change in Redpath's feelings about the tall, narrow house. It seemed to him that much of the sense of uncanniness which had oppressed him there could be put down to the unconscious turmoil caused by submerged memories trying to break through to the surface. As a child he had been terrified of dentists, and he was positive that such fear alone—suppressed, bottled up—had been sufficient to cloud his emotional reactions to the house. Many other things remained to be explained, but . . .

"I could enquire about the bicycle myself," Pardey said, "but if you're not there to claim it and take it away things'll start getting complicated."

"I suppose it would be better if I went with you and got it over with." Redpath stood up and, finding himself close to Leila, impulsively took her hand. "Leila, this can't have been much fun for you . . . listening to all my ramblings . . . I'm sorry it happened."

She gave him a warm, direct look. "Don't worry about that side of it. I'm glad you're all right."

"Not as glad as I am that *you're* all right." He turned his eyes upwards like an El Greco saint, causing her to smile, and the sight of the smile he had brought into being gave him an artist's sense of fulfilment.

"I want you back here at two o'clock sharp for a full set of psychometric tests," Nevison said, taking the cassette out of his tape machine. "That should give you time to go home if you want, and perhaps freshen up a little."

"Hint taken," Redpath replied, rasping the stubble on his chin. He left the office with Pardey amid inconsequential cross-talk and good-byes, filled with a rare conviction that life was all he could ask it to be, that it was good to pass through a dark tunnel now and again in order to appreciate properly the quality of the sunlight at the other end. The mood of euphoria was so pronounced that for a moment he had to consider the possibility that it was yet another psychotropic prelude, the deceiving sweet treachery of the falling sickness, but on analysis he decided the feeling was genuine and justified. He was an ordinary man, with no more than an ordinary man's share of failings and problems, and that was something to be celebrated. Half-way down the stair he paused and studied the bright green-and-cream checkerboard of the hall floor spread out beneath him, and it held reassuringly steady in his vision.

"What are you going to do about Tennent?" he said to Pardey

as the car began nosing its way into central Calbridge. "Do you have to arrest him on the spot?"

"You can relax on that score." Pardey gave him a quizzical glance. "I suppose you're another one who doesn't want to get involved in anything?"

"I admit it—I don't want to get involved."

"Well, you're already involved in this one to a small extent, but I'm going to slide you back out of it if I can—that's why I wanted you to come with me to collect your bicycle. As far as anybody in the house is concerned, I'll just be a friend who gave you a lift across town. With any luck I'll be able to get a good look at our man Tennent without any fuss."

"Then what?"

"Then I go back to the station and look at his mug shots and make sure it's the same man. Tennent is a fairly common name, you know. If I *don't* manage to see him now, I'll want you to call at the station later and look at some photographs. Okay?"

"That's all right," Redpath said, feeling relieved. "I don't mind doing that much."

"Any assistance short of actual help," Pardey murmured.

"Think nothing of it—just make sure they spell my name right on the medal." Redpath lapsed into silence, unable to decide whether he could warm to Pardey or not. The detective, in his capacity as Lcila's personal friend, had already saved him from what would have been a lengthy and difficult encounter with the police. It would be both ungrateful and unwise, he decided, to continue swapping the sort of banter which might develop into acrimony. He remained quiet until the redbrick canyon of the Woodstock Road had enfolded the car, then gave Pardey the final directions which brought them into Raby Street itself.

"Funny name to give a street," Pardey commented. "It doesn't make you think of Raby Castle or anything like that. Sounds too much like a disease."

"I suppose you're right." Redpath picked out the house numbered 131 in the foreshortening perspectives of the terrace on his left and watched it until the car had halted at the gateless gateway. The place looked even bleaker than he had expected, distinguished from the ordinary shabbiness of its neighbours by a dark and yawning quality about the windows which made it seem that light which entered the building was unable to get away again. Furry green caterpillars of moss clung between the old bricks, devouring the mortar with burrowing tendrils. Redpath, his gaze hunting across the dreary façade, experienced a sense of foreboding which somehow was unconnected with anything that had gone before.

"Let's get it over with," Pardey said, getting out of the car. Redpath joined him and they approached the outer door, the letterbox of which was held partly open by a crumpled advertising broadsheet. Pardey grasped the black-painted cast-iron knocker and beat vigorously on the door, sending thunderous percussions through the house's interior.

"Open up, madam," he said to Redpath, grinning. "I'm from *Homes And Gardens* and we want to feature you in our Christmas issue."

Redpath nodded and drew his lips into a smile. The house had sounded hollow. He crossed to the bay window, the curtains of which were almost fully drawn, put his face close to the glass and looked into the room where on the previous night he had sat for hours with the four members of his new "family". The room was completely empty of furniture, stripped to the bare floor boards. He began to feel cold.

"Get off your backside, madam," Pardey gritted, knocking more loudly than before, so loudly that a window frame vibrated. He locked eyes with Redpath, seemed to read something in his expression, then abruptly crouched and peered through the letterbox.

Redpath moved towards him. "Something funny seems to have . . ."

Pardey straightened up, his face savage. "Shut it, Redpath—just don't say *anything*!"

He took what appeared to be a piece of a white plastic ruler from his pocket, glanced around the deserted street, and slid the pliant strip into the door frame near the lock. Swearing impatiently, he made several forceful movements with his wrist and the brown-painted door swung open. The inner half-glazed door had been left ajar, revealing the naked hall floor and stair timbers of an uninhabited house. A breeze fluttered through an

106

accumulation of junk mail and circulars on the tiled floor of the porch.

Redpath placed the back of a hand on his forehead and fought to control the twitching of his lips. "This is where I was last night. I swear to God, that is the . . ."

"Look at the *dust*, man!" Pardey stepped into the porch and kicked a heavy envelope onwards into the hall. It slithered a short distance along the boards, making tracks in a thick and otherwise undisturbed layer of dust.

"Nobody has been in here for weeks," Pardey stated flatly.

Redpath looked about him with uncomprehending eyes and pointed at the leaded glass of the inner door. "There's the fleur-de-lis I talked about."

"Every house in the street probably has one of those bastards. Wait here."

Pardey strode to the staircase and went up it, stamping his feet to create maximum noise, and disappeared into the upper part of the house. His progress from room to room was punctuated by the slamming of doors. Redpath listened to him for a moment, still with his knuckles pressed to his forehead, then without any conscious volition walked towards the kitchen. He pushed open the door and surveyed the long bare room, noting the stained porcelain sink on the left, in the position he had expected. He turned to his right and looked behind the kitchen door. There was another door there, in the corner, and it was painted an incongruous fire-engine red. He raised the farm-house-type latch and pushed the door open. A maw of blackness widened beyond. Moving like a man trapped in a dream, he advanced to the first of the stone steps and tested the second one with his foot.

"That's all I need—for you to break your neck in here," Pardey said from close behind him. "Where's the light switch?"

There was a click as the detective operated a switch which Redpath had not seen because it was oddly located at the top of the door frame. A yellowish light came on in the cellar, illuminating a clean concrete floor. Pardey brushed past Redpath, clattered his way down the steps and examined the cellar. Redpath followed him almost to the foot of the steps and looked around the smoothly cemented walls.

So clean, he thought bemusedly. *Just like the one I dreamed about, the one in the American house. All it needs is a few pigeons that have been sandpapered to death.*

"Best part of the house, this," Pardey commented. "It looks like somebody was building a fall-out shelter." He turned and walked back up the steps, driving Redpath before him, turned off the light and closed the cellar door. Without speaking any further he shepherded Redpath through the brown dimness of the hall and out into the sunlit street, then pulled the outer door shut, sealing the house like a tomb. The bright, diamond-hard reality of street and sky imploded on Redpath from all directions, a stunning concentric shockwave which seemed to crush his skull.

"What are you doing?" he whimpered, lunging past Pardey to throw his weight against the door. "They can't do this to me! That's the house, I tell you—they're all in there!"

Pardey spun him around with practised roughness. "I'm going to do you one last favour, Monsignor—I'm going to let you walk away from here and get lost, and I'm going to pretend I never saw you. Also, I'm advising you to go to bed and sleep off whatever it is that's scrambling your brains."

"It's a trick," Redpath said distantly, scarcely moving his lips. "I tell you I was here last night."

"Son, you're not even here *now.*" Pardey flicked his fingers against Redpath's chest in contempt, walked to his car and looked back for a Parthian shot. "And you can tell Lady Leila that the next time she wants help she's to ring the Samaritans."

He got into the car and drove away, vanishing from sight at the nearest corner in only a few seconds, leaving Redpath alone and stranded at the centre of an alien universe.

CHAPTER 7

CALBRIDGE'S LEICESTER ROAD was at the heart of a self-consciously respectable district where trees, mature hedges and well-tended lawns were a dominant feature, and in which it was quite rare to see a pedestrian who was not exercising a dog. Redpath, even though he was freshly combed and shaved, felt conspicuous as he patrolled the section near the house where Leila lived. He was determined to meet her as she arrived home from work, and—in view of what had happened on his previous visit to the flat—had decided to be as transparent and ingenuous about it as possible. There was to be no lurking in shrubbery, no sudden emergence from shadows, nothing which might elicit a fear response.

With the approach of evening there had been a marked increase in the homeward flow of cars, their occupants scrutinising him in mechanised relays, but he maintained his vigil in the open until Leila's cherry-coloured mini, winking and slowing, separated itself from the other traffic. She saw him and began to raise one hand as the car disappeared between the brick piers of the house's front entrance. Redpath walked to the gateway, but remained outside the property line while Leila got out of the car. She closed the door, straightened up and shook out her hair in one fluid movement which struck Redpath as being peculiarly aristocratic, and which intensified his yearning to be with her.

Lady Leila, he thought. *Pardey was right, though he didn't know it. Lady Leila! If you'll marry me I'll even learn to play tennis and order Tanqueray's-and-tonic . . .*

"John Redpath!" Leila's face showed both exasperation and concern as she came towards him. "Where have you *been* all day?"

He smiled. "They seek him here, they seek him there."

"Why didn't you show up after lunch? Henry was ever so worried about you."

"I can imagine," Redpath said dryly.

"He telephoned Frank Pardey." Leila's gaze was direct, easily penetrating his manufactured nonchalance.

"So you've heard all about the empty house." He looked down and repeatedly kicked a small weed which was growing in a crack in the pavement, reducing it to a wet green strand which refused to be uprooted. "I'm supposed to have lost an entire day. Careless of me, wasn't it?"

"It's terrible for you, I know, but at least Henry is now convinced that Compound 183 is too dangerous to go on with in its present form."

"Henry is way behind the times," Redpath said, shaking his head as he obsessively pursued the sliver of vegetation with his foot. "It's no longer a question of drugs or hallucinations or side-effects. You see, I *know* that all those things I said happened yesterday actually did happen. There's no doubt or question about it—I know they happened."

Leila placed a sandalled foot over the remains of the weed, causing him to meet her gaze. "You have to face up to the evidence, John. For your own good."

"Evidence? You mean these new trousers and shirt I didn't have yesterday morning?"

"You could have bought them."

"I only had about three pounds in my pocket and I've still got most of that."

"That's not what I mean by evidence," Leila said, sadly but firmly. "You might simply have taken the clothes, or you might have got them some time previously."

"So my whole past goes down the drain, does it? Maybe I haven't actually got a past. Maybe I'm something they grew in a vat and programmed with fake memories."

"Please, John." Leila placed a restraining hand on his arm. "Would it help you to know that Henry and I went up to Raby Street this afternoon and looked at the house for ourselves? We didn't simply accept Frank Pardey's word."

"Did you? And what did you find?"

110

"The place was deserted and dusty. Nobody has lived there for ages."

"That's a great help to me," Redpath said bitterly. "Thanks a lot."

Leila changed the subject by looking about her in mock surprise. "Why are we standing out here?"

"I thought it might be better. After what happened, I didn't want to . . ."

"Don't be silly," Leila put in. "Are you coming up for coffee?"

"Yes, please." Redpath, feeling gratified, walked with her to the outside stairwell and ascended to the first landing. Leila opened the door with a key from her purse. The sight of the familiar sitting-room where only yesterday, as far as the evidence of memory was concerned, he had committed the ultimate obscenity touched Redpath with coolness, like the downdraft from an invisible wing. He went straight through into the kitchen and began filling the electric kettle.

"Is instant all right?" he called to Leila, who had stopped to examine her mail.

"You don't waste time making yourself at home, do you?"

"Everything's instant these days." Redpath plugged in the kettle and switched it on, set out two striped mugs and joined Leila in the living-room. The mere fact of her presence, her living presence, brought an upsurge of the joy he had experienced earlier, but with it came the realization that his ideas about recent "events" were very much like classical double-think. The only way he could cope with the memories was to classify them as what they proclaimed themselves to be—recollections of real people and real incidents—and yet only that morning he had been able to "remember" murdering Leila. To justify his mental processes it was necessary to become metaphysical and ascribe a vital quality of nightmare to some passages of memory, thus differentiating between them and the less remarkable sequences.

What's the underlying logic in that? Eh? Am I claiming that my mind has set up a nightmare factory which is happy to think up horror scenes, but refuses to waste its time making up ordinary events and ordinary people? Is that a union rule? And what's so ordinary about characters like Albert and . . ?

111

"I've just had a thought," he said. "When Henry rang your tame sleuth today, did they talk for long?"

"Quite a while—Frank can't decide whether he's been most abused by you, me or everybody."

"Did they discuss the fact that Wilbur Tennent, well-known figment of my imagination, is a real person with a real police record?"

"I think the conversation was too fraught for that kind of thing," Leila said. "But Tennent is a fairly common name—and you know what Henry would say."

Redpath nodded. "Unconscious data capture and retention. What if I went down to the cop shop and looked at all of Pardey's photos, and was able to pick out . . ? It doesn't make any difference, does it?"

"Unconscious capture and retention," Leila supplied, "and if you want to know something else that doesn't help—your horse came in first this afternoon."

"What horse?"

"Parsnip Bridge. Henry was intrigued by the name when he was running your tapes through, and he checked that there really was such a horse running today. It won at seven-to-one."

"Wilbur knew that would happen," Redpath said in a low voice, aware of icy heavings in the darkest pools of his mind. "Wilbur can see into the future. He opens the door before you knock."

"Don't elaborate the fantasy, John."

"What fantasy? I know damn all about horse racing, and I couldn't pick a winner to save my life. I didn't even know there *was* a horse called . . ."

"Unconscious capture and retention."

"That's a daft name for a horse," Redpath growled, shaking his head in despair.

"Poor John," Leila said, her lips quirking as she saw the expression on his face. "You're being put through the wringer and there's nothing I can do to help."

"You're helping me just by standing there," he assured her. "God, Leila, when I thought you were dead I wanted to . . ." Taken unawares by the stinging tears, he turned to go back to the kitchen, but she closed with him, looking into his face with a compassion which rendered her utterly beautiful.

"It's all right, John." Her eyes seemed luminous. "It helps to cry."

"Sounds like a good title for a song," he said, trying to take refuge in his jokey brand of cynicism, but his throat closed up so painfully on the last word that he had to wince. He looked down at her, chastened, dismayed by the possibility of his beginning to sob like a child.

"Come on." She took his hand and led him into the bedroom. He stood beside the bed, enjoying and being oddly comforted by the submissive role, while Leila closed the door and adjusted the Venetian blinds, reducing the light in the room to the mellowness of candle flames. Standing at the opposite side of the bed, she pointed at his jacket and began to unbutton her cardigan. They undressed in silent unison, garment for garment, reaching nudity at the same time. And when they lay down together the outside world faded from Redpath's consciousness like a dying star.

I could write yesterday off, you know. Pretend it never happened. What's so awful about losing a single day out of a lifetime? Ray Milland lost a whole week-end and it didn't do him any harm. Went from strength to strength, he did.

Redpath lay naked on the bed, watching Leila go about the room. His arms were folded behind his head, four pillows were arranged to give luxurious support to his back, and the relaxed state of his body was reflected in the meandering of his thoughts. He felt sane and secure, at times coming to terms with the idea that his mind was a master illusionist whose powers he had never suspected, at others speculating on the type of work he should try to obtain, or wondering how long Leila was going to let him stay with her on this visit. She had showered and now, clad only in underwear, was tidying the bedroom—an activity which made it easy for Redpath to imagine they were newly married and that life was always going to be as he saw it at that moment, an eternal springtime honeymoon, and endless stroll among the candled chestnuts of May.

That's all I want. More and more of the same. It's not too much to ask.

"This jacket looks as though it's been slept in," Leila said, lifting his brown zipper-up. "Isn't it about time you got it cleaned and pressed?"

He dismissed the idea with an airy flick of one foot. "It costs a fortune to have suede cleaned. They should have warned me about that in the shop when I bought it."

"Filling the pockets up with junk doesn't help it, either."

"Junk? *Junk?*" Looking at the garment's bulging pockets, Redpath was reminded that he had let most of yet another day go by without taking his standard dose of anti-convulsant. "Would you look in the right-hand pocket and see if there's a bottle of capsules in there?"

Leila put her hand in the pocket and brought it out filled with a medicine bottle, nail clippers, the lock and chain of Redpath's missing bicycle, a pencil stub, a plastic dispenser for dental floss, and a triangular piece of paper which looked as though it had been torn from a newspaper.

"Right, apologise for that remark about junk," Redpath said complacently. He was squirming into an upright position, preparatory to taking his Epanutin, when he saw that Leila was staring fixedly at the scrap of newsprint. Her expression was one of thoughtfulness, and of something else which caused a lurching sensation inside his chest.

"John?" Leila's voice was small and uncertain. "Where did you get this?"

"What is it?" He stood up and took the paper from her hand. As he had surmised, it was a piece torn from the corners of a newspaper, but the typography had an odd, slightly spidery appearance which he was unable to connect with any local publication. He looked at the dateline and saw that it read: *GILPINSTON BUGLE, TUESDAY, AUGUST 26, 1980.*

There was a moment of stillness during which Redpath could hear the ocean-booming of his own heart.

"I've already told you where I got this," he said, backing to the bed and sitting down, unable to take his eyes away from the single line of type. "Gilpinston, Illinois—I was there yesterday. I tried to snatch a newspaper and this piece must have come off in my hand."

"John, please don't . . ."

114

"How do you explain it, Leila? How do you explain this away?"

She sat down beside him and placed both hands on his forearm, holding tightly as though to give him anchorage. "John, please don't get it backwards. Didn't Henry predict that Gilpinston would turn out to be a real place? Didn't he say you must have seen the name somewhere and subconsciously noted it? That's why . . ."

"But look at the *date*, for Christ's sake!" Redpath held the scrap of paper close to her face. "That's yesterday's date! Don't you understand?"

"American papers are brought to England. Air travellers . . ."

Redpath cut in on her, half-shouting in his triumph. "From a small town in Illinois to a place like Calbridge! *On the same day!*"

Leila released his arm. "There's something wrong here."

"That's what I've been telling you all along." Redpath jumped to his feet and began pacing the room, driven by the force of the half-formed ideas which were spuming through his mind. "You know what this means, don't you? It's all so simple once you accept one or two new ideas. It means that Albert, tricky Albert, can move himself around just by thinking about it. Instantaneously, anywhere he wants. He did it out in the open the first time I saw him, and I didn't twig on. *Nobody* twigs on, because he goes around in an old boiler suit, and if he suddenly appears half-way along a street you automatically assume he got there by walking and you were too busy with your own thoughts to notice.

"And I'll tell you something else—he can take people with him! That's how I got to Gilpinston and back yesterday afternoon. Albert did it. I don't think he likes me. He wanted to scare hell out of me, and it worked. My God, it worked."

Redpath could hear his own words pouring out faster and faster, the sentences becoming shorter and more choppy as the time available for consideration of each new thought grew less. He had a feeling of no longer being in control, of instinct racing ahead of reason, but there was nothing he could do about it. His movements became jerky and frenetic.

"I tell you, Leila, Henry Nevison is wasting his time at the

115

Jeavons. He should be up in Raby Street if he wants to study parapsychology. That house! I said it was a rest home for freaks, but I didn't realise how close I was to . . . They've all got something. Something different. Albert can teleport people. Take Wilbur Tennent—he's a clairvoyant. Precognition. Miss Connie is a bit like Albert, but she does it with objects. Psycho-kinesis, they call it. PK. Apportation.

"Then there's Betty York. I don't know what she . . . yes, I do! She's the physical component of the whole set-up. She's what Henry would call the soma. She looks after the others, and makes sure they get fed and so forth. And she does other jobs, too. I didn't just bump into her in the park yesterday—she came out to get me. On purpose! I'm as big a freak as any of them. I'm a telepath—and the house was short of one telepath. Maybe he died. I'll bet that Prince Reginald character lived there, the one Wilbur is wanted for questioning about, and I'll bet you he died, and I'll bet you I was his replacement . . .

"The capsules, Leila! Hand me the capsules!" The sight of Leila's face, pale and worried, gave Redpath a powerful jolt as he took the brown bottle from her outstretched hand, and all at once the nervous overload seemed to drain from his body. Smiling weakly, he sat down beside her on the edge of the bed and opened the bottle with trembling fingers. He felt cold and ill.

"I'm all right," he said, putting a capsule into his mouth and swallowing it. "Don't be afraid."

"I'm not afraid."

"You reckon this crazy spell will soon pass."

She gave him an unconvincing smile. "It already has."

"Leila," he said, slowly and gently, "I believe every word of what I've just said. I don't understand all of it, but I believe it. In one of the nightmares I dreamt the house was a living thing and the cellar was its stomach . . . That's ridiculous, of course, but the analogy is there just the same. The house and those people in it are like a composite being—and they want me to join the family. I think now that *they* made me believe I had murdered you, just so that I'd be driven to go into hiding with them, though I don't know how they did it. Maybe there's a member of the family I haven't met yet, but the point is that it was all part of a plan. Don't you see that?"

116

"I don't want you to get upset," Leila said unhappily.

"I'm not upset. I feel a lot better now I've got some idea of what's been going on. It all makes sense of a kind when you think about it. A group like that, each member with one special talent, can really look after itself—and that's why the house was empty when I got there this morning with Pardey. Wilbur would have known we were coming, you see. He gave the warning and Albert moved out all the people and Miss Connie moved out all the furniture and other stuff. And it wouldn't have been hard for somebody like her to blanket the place with dust and make it look as though nobody had been there for ages."

Leila made to stand up, but Redpath caught her wrist and continued to speak in an abstracted monotone. "I'll bet you they're all in the States at this very minute, living in that other house, the one with the same layout as the place in Raby Street—but what's it all in aid of? What brought them all together in the first place, and what do they want with me? What makes them run?"

Have they ever sandpapered anybody to death?

"John, you've got to unwind and think things over calmly," Leila said. "Why don't you lie down again and perhaps have a doze? You must be tired out."

Redpath considered the proposition. "I daresay it would be safe for me to go to sleep. If they're thousands of miles away they probably won't feed me any bad dreams."

"The rest would be good for you." Leila stood up, rearranged the pillows and gently pushed him down on to them. He eyed her appreciatively and, as she was leaning over to cover him with a sheet, lightly pinched the tiny roll of fat which had appeared just below her navel. She pushed his hand away, went to a wardrobe and selected a lime green dress which enhanced the colour of her hair. It was only when she had put on white sandals and was looking around for her purse that it dawned on Redpath that she had been preparing to go out. He found the idea strangely annoying.

"What are you doing, Leila?" He raised himself on one elbow. "You're not going out, are you?"

"Just to get some butter and one or two other things—I wasn't expecting a lodger."

117

He glanced at his watch. "But it's nearly eight o'clock."

"The shops in Botanic Avenue will still be open."

"I don't want you to rush around getting food for me."

"It's no trouble. I can be back in . . ."

"I don't want you to go out, Leila." Redpath, now sitting upright, realised he had spoken too sharply and tried to make amends. "It's selfish of me, I know, but . . ."

"It's all right, darling," she said quickly, "I can manage without going shopping—as long as you don't mind margarine on your toast."

Redpath nodded, mollified. "I don't mind margarine."

"It's supposed to be better for your health, anyway," Leila said in a subdued voice. She sat down at her dressing table and began to work on her cuticles with an orange stick.

Unable to suppress a feeling that something had gone wrong, Redpath stared at her in silence as he went over the events of the previous ten minutes, like a hunter backtracking to pick up a lost trail. The atmosphere had been harmonious up to the moment when he had half-deduced and half-guessed the underlying facts about the house in Raby Street and its effect on his life, but since then . . .

"Leila," he said gravely, "it has just occurred to me—you've really taken all this in your stride, haven't you?"

She lowered her head, concentrating her attention on her fingernails. "I don't know what you mean."

"I mean all that stuff I told you about those people up in Raby Street. It was pretty astonishing. In fact, it was *very* astonishing— but you don't seem astonished."

"I . . . Perhaps I haven't fully taken it in."

He weighed up her reply for several seconds. "You don't believe any of it do you? You think I'm mad. You were trying to humour me."

Leila's shoulders slumped momentarily, then she turned to look at him with haunted eyes. "John, you've got one piece torn off a newspaper, and that's all there is. One piece of a newspaper!"

"An American newspaper."

"There might be half-a-dozen Gilpinstons in this country, and even if it *is* an American newspaper—what of it? Have you considered that it might be a weekly newspaper, printed days in advance?"

Redpath had not thought of that possibility, but he dismissed it as being irrelevant. "All that matters is that I was able to produce physical evidence for something that people said had only happened in my imagination. Can't you see what that meant to me?"

"I saw what it did to you."

"Fair comment." Some quirk in Redpath's mental make-up made him feel oddly uplifted by the challenge implicit in Leila's remark. "You're a rational person, and—not having experienced all that I experienced yesterday at first hand—you require more evidence. There's nothing wrong with that, nothing at all." He spoke pleasantly, slipping into a near-imitation of Henry Nevison's best professorial manner. "Now, what other evidence can I produce to strengthen my case? Intriguing little problem, isn't it?"

Instead of being amused, Leila eyed him with something which could have been desperation. "John, do you realise what you're saying? Do you remember what you told us in the office this morning, the part about finding two flayed bodies in the bath in that house? Are you going to try proving that really happened, as well?"

Redpath's confidence wavered. "Was that not in the nightmare? It's getting hard to keep track of what was real and what was . . ." He looked about him with narrowed eyes, fighting against the swarming sensation inside his head, and his gaze fixed itself on Leila's bedside telephone. A strange idea was born in his mind, an idea which struck him as all the more bizarre in the context because it was entirely practical. He picked up the phone, dialled for the operator and asked to be put through to the international directory enquiry service.

Leila set her orange stick aside. "What are you doing?"

"It's all right," he said in sudden manic glee. "I'll pay for the call. Give me a pen or something—quickly!" He took the eyebrow pencil she handed him and gestured for silence as the connection was made. In little more than a minute he had written the telephone number of the *Gilpinston Bugle* across the skin of his right knee.

"There we are," he said triumphantly, indicating the dark sprawl of numerals. "You wanted proof, and proof is what you're going to get."

Leila came towards him. "I asked what you were doing."

"Just listen to this—Illinois is five or six hours behind us, so it should be mid-afternoon there." He dialled the international code for the United States, followed by the number of the *Bugle,* and the call was answered almost immediately. "My name is John Redpath and I'm calling from England," he said in a businesslike voice. "Tell me, please—is the *Bugle* a daily newspaper?"

"Yes, sir. We publish six days a week." The voice of the switchboard girl was clear in the bedroom. "Can I help you?"

"There was no need to make an international call to prove that," Leila whispered furiously. "There are newspaper directories in the . . ."

Redpath held one finger to his lips and spoke into the phone. "I have an interesting story for your paper—could you put me through to a reporter, please?" He grinned at Leila during the brief wait, filled with a heady confidence in his own ability.

"Reporters' room, Dave Knight speaking," a male voice said with some diffidence. "Did you say you were calling from England, Mr Redpath?"

"Yes, indeed. I'm connected with the Jeavons Institute, Calbridge, which is a research offshoot of the University College of South Haverside. My department is researching some aspects of E.S.P., and something interesting has just cropped up which—believe it or not—has a direct link with Gilpinston, Illinois."

"Did you say E.S.P.?" The voice was alert now.

Redpath winked at Leila. "That's what I said."

"Is there someone from Gilpinston working on this research?"

"It's more interesting than that, Dave, as I think you'll agree. The reason I'm calling you is that one of our subjects swears he has projected his consciousness into a house in Gilpinston. Visited it yesterday without actually going there in the flesh, if you know what I mean."

"Are we talking about something like an astral body?"

"Something like that, although we wouldn't use that particular term. The point is that our subject has given us a precise description of the house and the street it's in. We have no way of knowing how much of this is just his imagination, but if the details *did* happen to check out you would have a very nice little offbeat story on your hands. What do you think?"

There was a pause. "It would be a nice story if I could be sure it wasn't some kind of a hoax, Mr Redpath. I'm not implying anything, but . . ."

"No, no! You're right to be sceptical—I'm sceptical myself. I'll give you my number here in England so that you can call me back, and I'll also give you Professor Nevison's number at the institute. You could speak to him there tomorrow and confirm everything before you go into print. Of course, if you'd prefer that I went to some other paper . . ."

"No, I don't want you to do that, Mr Redpath—I'm very glad you rang us first. Now, did you say you had an exact address in Gilpinston?"

"The street is 13th Avenue S.E. and the house number is 2224. Does that sound feasible?" Receiving an affirmative, Redpath went on to describe the house, mentioning that the owner's name could be Rodgers, and giving every significant detail he could recall—pale blue front door, diagonal line of metal numerals, fire hydrant immediately outside, Gruber's Delicatessen at the corner, a bar known as Pete's Palace next door . . . He concluded by stating Leila's telephone number and saying he would wait for a return call.

"Okay, it won't take me long to drive out to 13th Avenue and check this out," Knight said. "Is there anything else?"

"Well . . ." Redpath hesitated, sensing that he was going too far, introducing an unaccountable element of danger, but Leila's earlier remark had implanted a nagging doubt about the blurring of the line between reality and nightmare. "I don't want to give you the subject's name at this stage, but there was something about the bathroom in the house, something frightening that he didn't want to talk about. I don't even know why I'm mentioning this—you'll hardly be going right into the house, will you?"

"It all depends," Knight said, the dubious note returning to his voice. "You have to play this sort of thing by ear."

"I'll look forward to hearing from you." Redpath set the

121

phone down and got up to face Leila, who was standing with her hands on her hips in what was almost a caricature of outrage. His feeling of manic elation had ebbed, but in its place was a comforting sense of having taken a positive action, no matter how slight, against the forces of chaos and unreason. It had been his first opportunity to strike back.

"You'd no right to do that, John Redpath," Leila said, her eyes brilliant with anger. "What's Henry going to say if the newspapers do pick this up? Do you realise the position he could be in?"

"Do you think I'm enjoying this?" Redpath reached for his shirt and began getting dressed. "Do you think I'm having fun?"

"Perhaps not, but . . ."

"*Perhaps* not! Leila, I'm trying to fight my way back into the human race. I'm all alone in this thing, but if that reporter calls back and says those details have checked out . . . Well, somebody will have to sit up and take notice, that's all."

"What if it works the other way?" Leila said. "What if the other place doesn't exist?"

He gave her a wry smile. "Then I'll know I was bombed out of my mind all day yesterday. I'll just have to take it from there."

"Promise?"

"Don't even need to promise—I wouldn't go against the facts."

"In that case, do you want a green salad or a potato salad with your chicken?" Leila said, with a visible change of mood.

Redpath understood at once that she was anticipating a negative report from Dave Knight, and that she would prefer not to discuss the subject in the meantime. The idea of a truce, of a return to normal living—no matter how temporary—had an undeniable attraction for him, and he readily entered into the game.

"Green salad," he said, "but I want to mix my special Italian dressing for it. This new recipe I've got doesn't just stimulate the taste buds—it makes them roam up and down your tongue in armed gangs demanding more and more."

Leila went to the door. "Why do you always exaggerate?"

122

"Have you ever seen a mob of taste buds in a threatening mood?" he said, following her into the kitchen. "A fearsome sight!"

He helped Leila prepare a simple evening meal, and while they were eating it discovered that one of his favourite films—a 1944 comedy-thriller called *Scared Stiff*, starring Jack Haley—was having a rare showing on television. Leila agreed to watch it with him, and while they sat together in the companionable dusk, laughing at the same things that people had laughed at in another time and place, building bridges, he found himself wishing that the telephone would not ring. He wanted to rest for a while. He was tired of arguing and being afraid, and of struggling to assimilate concepts which were alien to the world-view which had sustained him since infancy, and there was a magical peacefulness in being able to lie back on a deep settee beside the woman he loved while darkness drifted down from the sky and there was no need to resist being drawn into the beguiling little universe of the cathode ray tube, where Jack Haley's face periodically floated in space . . . a comet . . . a comic comet . . . a comic comet rendering him comatose . . .

Redpath slipped easily and cleanly into sleep.

Some miles away, on the far side of Calbridge, the blue-white street lights had begun to glow all along the redbrick canyon of the Woodstock Road, casting unnatural shadows, producing odd changes in the apparent colours of people's clothes and cars. Buses were still plying the road—compact, mobile constellations of yellow stars—and further salients were carved into the darkness by the lights of the corner shops; honey-coloured in the case of the confectioners, tobacconists, fish-and-chippers, and the old-style public houses; cold, motionless fluorescent white in the case of those building society branches, estate agencies and utilities stores whose fronts were illuminated all night to encourage window-shoppers and deter thieves. Traffic lights added their contributions of ruby, topaz and emerald to the slim chain of radiance, and would continue to do so all through the night, patiently orchestrating the flow and counter-flow of vehicles which existed only in the proto-minds of their automatic control boxes.

It would never really get dark on the Woodstock Road, but from a comparatively early hour night held full sway in the narrow tributaries which disgorged into it. The lamps were feebler and much further apart in those lesser streets. Some of the lights had fallen into disrepair without attracting the attention of the council's engineering and maintenance departments, others had been vandalised for pleasure or with an eye to clandestine profit. It was only necessary to walk a hundred yards from the main road, and perhaps make a couple of turns, to enter a black region where pedestrians were few. Those who did venture out at night tended to walk quickly, with their heads down, and to keep themselves to themselves.

And there was nobody at all abroad in Raby Street, nobody to pay any attention or to pass any comment, when lights suddenly began to glimmer behind the curtains of the house with the numerals 131 above its blistered brown door.

For a moment Redpath was looking down at an expanse of green-and-cream floor tiles and he feared the nightmare had begun again, but this time there was a qualitative difference in the experience. He was able to interpret the visual pattern almost immediately, and he knew with utter certainty that the radiant squares were part of a huge machine.

The display panel of a computer and the instrumentation of an aircraft were the nearest parallels he could envisage, but the engineering principles employed here were far removed from anything which had originated in human minds. It was likely that information was being presented, and yet both form and content were unintelligible to Redpath. There were signs of continuous, furtive movement beneath some of the translucent slabs, and he knew that its origins were neither mechanical nor electronic—the machine incorporated living organic components which served it in ways beyond his understanding.

The complex image held steady before him—not a memory, not an illusion, not a dream.

This is a reality. It isn't my reality, but it's a reality nevertheless, and I'm sharing it.

As had happened before, a brown slurry surged across the glowing checkerwork, like a tide of clotting blood, and in places

124

the light from brighter panels shone upwards through it with the redness of port wine, revealing a thready internal structure. At the advancing edge of the mass there was a constant agitation of pseudopods which probed and tested the surface before filling out with dark fluids and being reabsorbed. But Redpath felt no fear, no revulsion.

That is part of my body, in this reality. I am a Thrice-born, in this reality, and I have travelled far in pursuit of a Once-born, an abomination who sought to break the decreed cycle of ingestion, purification and renascence. He committed the ultimate crime against my kind, the crime of permitting his bioplasm to degenerate with age. The disease, for that is what he has become, must be eradicated because it would be almost as great a crime to allow such malignancy to exist.

I have been scry-sensing for him very carefully during these latter years of the pursuit, in this reality, and I know that he is injured, or that the process of degeneration has greatly advanced, because he has not made use of his higher powers in all that time. He must, therefore, be close to his ship. It will be sufficient to locate the ship . . .

As had happened before, four squares near the centre of the vari-coloured pattern grew darker and merged into one, taking on the semblance of a transparent hatch which covered a well of night. But now the blackness was far from complete. It formed the background and setting for the brilliant blue-white disc of a planet which was quickly identifiable as Earth. The planet was growing close.

It will be sufficient to locate the ship, and then . . .

Something bad happened to Redpath.

There was a *loosening*, a flicker-shifting of geometries. The image before him twitched and altered its colours and proportions, and suddenly he was at a remove from that reality, and the thoughts he had been share-thinking—cold, ascetic, dispassionate—were obliterated in a vortex of dark emotions. Fear mingled with hatred, anger and contempt, but the fear was ever dominant, engulfing him in a writhing, raging blackness which was shot through with memory fragments, partial images, shards of an unimaginably alien existence. For an instant that life was congruent with Redpath's life.

125

He began to scream.
NO! NO! NO! NO! NO!

Redpath was running in a twisted corridor. The corners were sharp and difficult to negotiate at speed, and his progress was further hindered by the fact that the corridor had been designed to resemble a series of connected rooms, such as would be found in an ordinary dwelling. There was a hall, a kitchen and a living-room—endlessly repeated—and in the living-room was a television set which shone in the dimness like a miniature stained glass window. Close to the television was a girl who sat huddled on a settee, rocking backwards and forwards in terror, her hands covering her face. He became aware of the faint sounds of her distress, then there came the shock of recognition, a sense of guilt and responsibility.

"Leila?" Redpath clung to the jamb of the kitchen door, less for support than to quell the remnants of a blind instinct to flee. "Don't cry, Leila—I know it all now. I know *everything*."

She continued to cower, to make herself as small as possible.

He crossed the room, turned off the television and knelt in front of her. "Don't cry, Leila. We've both got things to do, and there's very little time. Look at me, please."

She raised her head slowly. Her face was wan and miserable, robbed of beauty, and he knew at once that the first vital step in his plan would be to calm her down and restore her confidence in him. The necessary task which lay ahead of Leila Mostyn was even more demanding than his own in some ways, and she would be unable to face it unless he armed her with knowledge and trust.

"Don't be afraid of me," he whispered. "I got a bad shock, but I'm all right now and we've got to talk. Will you listen to me for a while and try to understand what I'm saying, no matter how fantastic it might seem? Will you?"

"What is it, John?" Her lips seemed to be numb, scarcely moving as she spoke.

He took a deep breath. "I said some incredible things today, and nobody would believe me—and then I came up with concrete proof. Just remember that and trust me and hear me out. The telepathy project was more successful than any of us

126

expected, Leila—the fact is that I've been in mental contact with beings from another planet. Does that sound too fantastic for words?"

"Not if you say so."

"Good! We're making progress. The next thing to understand is that these beings are totally unlike anything you've ever seen. They don't look like us and they don't think like us. Their bodies are soft, almost entirely liquid. They can flow like syrup, or jam that hasn't set, but that doesn't stop them being intelligent and having a social structure. Are you still with me?

"The contact I made didn't last long, but it was clear—too clear—and I know that their society is based on a form of cannibalism. When an individual reaches a certain age he allows himself to be eaten or absorbed by a younger being, and somehow he seems to survive the experience and be reborn or reincarnated. Though maybe he doesn't really survive it. Maybe it's a matter of faith with them, like a religion, and that could be where the trouble started—I think I'd be inclined to run away when my time came round. Maybe I ought to feel some sympathy for that thing in Raby Street."

Leila started visibly and made to turn away, but he put a hand under her chin and forced her to continue looking at him.

"He ran away, Leila. And a long time ago—twenty or thirty years ago, perhaps even during the war—he came down on Earth, probably falling at random, and I don't think I need to spell out exactly where. A couple of houses have been chopped out of the row behind Raby Street, and I'd say that's where his ship went in. The damage could have been put down to a bomb, or maybe a gas explosion, and nobody has ever had any reason to suspect otherwise or dig deep underneath.

"That's how it all started, but you can't understand what's been going on all these years unless you know more about these aliens. They've got psi powers, Leila. Their bodies are pretty useless as machines, but they compensated by evolving a whole range of talents that enabled them to beat the competition—telepathy, psychokinesis, precognition, other abilities that we haven't even got names for. Mental control of animals is one of them, and it was probably developed for feeding purposes. Tele-hypnosis, you might call it, though I doubt if . . ."

127

"John, can we have some tea?" Leila said, her throat vibrating in his fingers. "This is all so . . . I'd love some tea."

"Good idea." He made his voice warm and encouraging, anxious to demonstrate that he was entirely rational and reasonable, and in that way give extra credence to his words. A sense of desperate urgency was pounding at the doors of his mind, but nothing could be done until Leila was fully convinced and won over. He stood back, allowing her to rise, and then followed her into the kitchen. She looked cold and tired as she filled the electric kettle. He resolved to proceed with even greater care.

"The mental control aspect is one of the things that scares me most, because it's so insidious. There's no way of telling how deep and how far back it goes, but we know this alien is intelligent and devious, and it's been drawing up its plans for a long time. A dentist used to have that house in Raby Street—now, did he choose it by accident, merely because it was suitable for his needs and the district hadn't yet declined at that time? Or was he influenced in his decision because a dentist's surgery draws in a lot of people and the thing that was waiting under the ground wanted access to as many minds as possible?

"I was in that house when I was a kid—is that anything to do with my developing a vestige of telepathic ability? Is that why I volunteered for the screening tests at the Jeavons? And you heard Henry Nevison suggest that the house had been used by a dentist—is that what led to his interest in parapsychology in the first place?

"How many local bigwigs, who might otherwise have blocked an off-beat research project in a place like the Jeavons, were manipulated into going along with it? And what about all the people who live nearby? Is their natural curiosity damped down in some way so that they pay no attention to odd activities?"

Leila set out cups and saucers, then opened a lacquered tin and brought out a rectangular madeira cake. She looked around, strangely hesitant, took a long knife from the wall rack and began to cut the cake into thin slices, working with painstaking care.

"I don't understand that part," she said, in something like her normal tones. "What would be the point of all that mind-control and manipulation?"

128

"Life or death—it's as simple as that. Our visitor is being hunted by another member of its own race, a killer with a spectrum of senses you and I can't even visualize, and it had to lie low. For a human fugitive that could mean not moving or making a sound; for the monster we're talking about it meant not using many of its natural abilities. The problem was that it couldn't survive *without* those abilities, so what did it do? How did it get out of the dilemma?"

Leila paused in her meticulous slicing of the cake. "By using substitutes."

"Exactly right," Redpath said, encouraged. For minutes he had been listening to his own voice with growing dismay and wondering if any person who had not been directly involved could ever believe a story of such extravagance. He had set out to soothe and coax Leila into acceptance, then it had seemed to him that his calmness was defeating its own purpose, that it would have been right and appropriate for him to give way to his dread, to howl out to all the world his foreknowledge of the fact that the megadeaths were coming and there was very little time in which to do anything about it. Leila, however, was responding better than he had at first anticipated, and it appeared he was getting his message across to her.

"Exactly right," he repeated. "That's what the people in that house really are—substitutes, stand-ins, prosthetics. That's the common factor I was looking for. You can see how they all work together, each one serving in his or her own way and allowing the . . . the puppet master to remain in hiding. The hunter has no interest in human beings and our activities, even our rare paranormal activities, apparently don't register with it. And that other thing has been living under the house in Raby Street for years, decades, using human beings the way we use pack animals and discarding them when they become useless."

"Without anybody noticing?"

"It tries hard to be inconspicuous—and it's done a bloody good job over the years considering that we're as alien to it as it is to us. The concept of the family unit must be completely foreign to it, but it tries to present the outside world with the right sort of picture. They have a sing-song in the front parlour every night, and everybody smiles and looks happy, and Miss

E 129

Connie knits the way an old lady is supposed to, but she doesn't knit anything in particular. She just knits. I had one night of that, Leila, but the others have been going through it for years, night after night after night . . ."

Redpath paused, momentarily distracted. "Did you ever think of hell as a shabby old room, with rexine armchairs and luncheon meat sandwiches, where you're not allowed to scream in case you disturb the neighbours?"

Leila toyed thoughtfully with the knife. "It's hard to credit that a group of people could be held and controlled that way against their wills."

"But it's *true*, Leila—though I've a feeling it isn't an entirely straightforward or consistent effect. I think you have to get within close range of the beast in the early stages. That's why Betty York was sent out to bring me to the house any way she could. If you ask me, Albert is the only one who might be awkward at times. I'm nearly sure he . . . what do they call it in that kids' TV show? . . . 'jaunts' over to the States every now and then just to buy American cigarettes. Possibly he would be the hardest one to control because of the way he can flit about. There's that business of whipping me off to the house in Gilpinston with him—I'll bet you that was a nasty little trick of his own. He wanted to . . ."

Redpath hesitated again, frowning. "You were right about the bodies in the bathtub, Leila. That wasn't in the nightmare, was it? It must have really happened, but why would anybody want to peel dead bodies? There must be something I don't . . ." He stopped speaking as a familiar but loathsome sensation manifested itself behind his eyes. There was a slithering coldness in his brain. Inside his head was a worm, a giant worm which had begun to coil and uncoil.

"There's something I still don't understand." Leila turned to face him, still casually holding the long knife. "If you were in that house, fully under the thing's control, how did you break free?"

Redpath pressed both hands to his temples and gave her a numb, lop-sided smile. "Can't you guess? I thought that part was obvious." He swayed slightly as the disturbance in his mind intensified, and when he spoke again his voice was pitched unnaturally high. "I've been wasting time . . . thought I was safe . . . I'm needed, you see . . . it needs me to give warning—just before the bomb comes . . . the Thrice-born is going to bomb the ship, and he'll use a big bomb, an area weapon . . . there'll be no more England, Leila . . . perhaps no more Europe . . ."

He made a shuddering intake of breath, staring at Leila as though seeing her for the first time, and fought to control the spasmodic twitching which had developed in the muscles around his mouth. "Here's what you've got to do, Leila. That house in Gilpinston is the bolt-hole, and that's why it's so far away. Seconds before the bomb explodes . . . just before the big bang . . . the thing, the puppet master, will be taken there by Albert. After the bomb explodes there'll be complete silence. Scry-silence, I mean. The Thrice-born will wait for a time, listening, but there'll be complete silence, and he'll go away again, satisfied.

"I'll probably be dead, too—because the puppet master won't take the risk of my somehow revealing it's still alive, but you can prevent all that. You and I working together can prevent all that—by killing the puppet master before the bomb is dropped. The Thrice-born will know what has happened. He'll scry-sense it and he won't drop the bomb. At least, I don't think he will. You'll help me, won't you, Leila? *Say you'll help me, for Christ's sake!"*

Redpath lurched forward and grabbed Leila by the shoulders, crooking his fingers deep into the soft flesh. She flinched and her lips moved silently as she thrust the knife into him. The pain was a shocking, sickening admixture of every other pain he had known. Retaining his grip on Leila's shoulders, he looked down at the knife. It had gone through his shirt and penetrated some distance into the gathering of subcutaneous fat just above his belt, but the thrust had been checked at that point. Leila, still gripping the handle of the knife, was locked in a trembling rigidity.

"You didn't mean to do that," he said gently, almost benignly, taking the blade from her and drawing it clear of his own body. "I frightened you, and you reacted out of fear, and we're not going to let a minor incident like that affect our plans, are we?"

"No, John." Leila's voice was virtually inaudible and tears glistened on her cheeks. "I'm sorry I . . ."

"Good girl!" Redpath set the knife down, tore a handful of kitchen tissue from the wall-mounted roller and tucked it inside his shirt, forming a loose pad in the region of the wound. Blood had been channelled along the top of his belt, creating a broad horizontal stain across his waist. He applied pressure to the pad with his left forearm and turned his attention back to Leila. The geyser of pain seemed to have had a purging scouring effect within his head, but the intangible pressures had increased immeasurably. Something had been thwarted, and now it was impatient and angry.

"Can't talk much longer," he said in whispered panic. "It wants to listen. Don't take time to pack a bag, Leila—just get your passport and credit cards and all the money you have. If you leave now you can be at London Airport soon after midnight. With luck you'll be able to get a walk-on flight to Chicago before morning. As soon as you get there find some . . ."

"Chicago!" Leila backed away from him, shaking her head. "I can't."

"*Don't argue!*" Redpath's voice was thunderous in the confined space of the kitchen, and his gaze alternated wildly between Leila's face and the knife which was lying beside the sink. "Why are you arguing? You *bitch*! What are you trying to do?"

"John, I . . ." Leila stared at him for a moment, eyes flaring white, then turned and ran into the living-room.

Redpath—swearing dementedly, his limbs rigid with fury— picked up the knife and went after her.

CHAPTER 8

THE MINI'S ENGINE, powered by a new battery, turned over
with all the scrabbling eagerness of a terrier going after a rat,
shaking the framework of the vehicle with its energy, but the
ignition sequence refused to sustain itself. Alarmed by the
engine's perversity, Leila Mostyn kept turning the key and pump-
ing the accelerator pedal until a listless note amid the mechanical
frenzy told her she had flooded the system. She paused, trying to
breathe steadily, and looked back over her shoulder towards the
house. The lights were on in the narrow outside stairwell, and at
any second she could expect to see the tall, lurching, stoop-
shouldered, bleak-eyed apparition that had once been John Redpath bounding down the concrete steps. It was a vision which
threatened to undermine what was left of her self-control. She
bit her lower lip, forced herself to count slowly to sixty and tried
the starter again. The engine fired into healthy life.

She switched on the lights, swerved the car out through the
gates into the Leicester Road and drove towards the town centre.
Her intention was to go straight to the Calbridge police station,
but at a distance of a hundred yards from the house—encased in
a mobile metal shell which gave her the ability to outpace the
devil himself—the crushing sense of fear abated slightly and old
modes of thought began to reassert themselves. She *knew* John
Redpath and, regardless of what had happened to him or had
been done to him, the notion of handing him over to the author-
ities to be restrained and sedated and mentally dissected seemed
like the ultimate act of betrayal. He was insane, frighteningly
insane—so much so that in one hideous moment of panic she
had almost sunk a knife into his body—but it had to be a
temporary condition, caused by the treatment he had received
at the institute.

133

Henry Nevison would know what to do, she decided. Henry could give the best advice, would have all the right polysyllabics on tap. *Should Compound 183 prove to have psychosomimetic properties* . . . And so on, and so on.

At the thought of being able to transfer her burden of responsibility to Nevison's shoulders, where it properly belonged, Leila reduced the car's speed, and at once other considerations came into her mind. If she brought the police in now there would be an immediate explosion of scandal—the story the media would noise abroad would be a sensational cocktail of strange Karloffian experiments, madness, flying saucers, and blood-letting in a suburban love nest—and it would be harmful to everybody who was directly or indirectly involved. The repercussions would reach as far as her own parents down in Pangbourne.

A fresh decision made, she turned left at the next intersection and went left again so that she was driving back the way she had come on an avenue which ran parallel to Leicester Road. At the first cross-street above her starting point she made another left turn, drove slowly to the end of the street and halted almost at the corner in a position from which she could observe the entrance to her apartment house. She switched off the car's lights but left the engine running, unwilling to risk the consequences of perhaps being noticed by John when he emerged and not being able to take flight in time. His sudden lunatic rages in the flat had been terrifying enough, but she sensed they would be as childish tantrums compared to what he would do on learning she was not at that moment speeding on her way to Gilpinston, via London Airport and Chicago.

Leila gave an involuntary shudder and drew her coat closer together at her throat as she recalled those last few minutes alone with John in the apartment . . . his abrupt descent into total irrationality . . . the brandishing of the knife as he followed her about in search of her passport . . . the incoherence and the wild ramblings . . .

Remember the address, Leila . . . I can beat the puppet master, but it doesn't know that . . . go straight to Gilpinston . . . the Thrice-born is too close . . . hire a car if you need one . . . fill the bottles with petrol and stop up the necks with rags . . . I can break the control, but the Once-born doesn't know . . . both

134

*houses have to go up at the same time . . . we can kill it, Leila . . .
midnight tomorrow night—that's seven o'clock in Illinois . . .
don't worry—the bottles won't explode in your hand . . . have
faith, just have faith in me . . . light the rags and throw the
bottles through the front windows . . . the Thrice-born will know
what has happened . . .*

And then as a final touch of unreason, ludicrous and inexplicable, there had been the business with her television set. He had
tinkered with the small controls at the back of the set until he
had identified the vertical hold adjuster, then had shown it to her
and had made her kneel down and grip the knurled projection.
He had switched the set on, turned his back to it and covered
his eyes with both hands, and had ordered her to rotate the
control until the television picture was far out of adjustment,
rolling upwards so quickly that it was almost impossible to guess
what was on the screen.

Is it rolling? His voice had been timid. *I'm afraid to look.*

At that moment, and only for a moment, her pity for him had
almost overcome the sense of fear that was yammering through
the molecular corridors of her nervous system. He had looked
and sounded bemused—as childishly vulnerable as she had sometimes known him to be when faced with an unexpected challenge
—and she had dared hope that the dark shadow was lifting from
his mind. But within a second of the set being switched off he
had dragged her to the entrance of the flat and had thrown her
on to the landing. His face had been distorted, inhuman.

Run, Leila! For God's sake . . . for all our sakes . . . RUN!

As she gazed into the night-time stillness of the suburban road,
at the receding row of gateway pillars and the trees whose leaves
had been turned into Yuletide plastic by the intervening street
lights, Leila began to wonder if she ought to have set off to
Henry Nevison's house. She had seen John struggling into his
suede jacket and had concluded that he was about to leave—but
was any logical deduction valid in his case? Several minutes had
gone by since her escape and it appeared that he was still in the
flat. She tightened her grip on the steering wheel and had given
the accelerator a tentative jab when there was a movement on
the opposite side of the road.

John Redpath emerged into the light and turned in the

direction of the town. He was walking slowly, like an elderly man, and had his left arm pressed to his side. In his right hand he was carrying a case-like object which she had to look at twice before recognising it as her portable television. With shoulders hunched and head lowered, apparently oblivious to his surroundings, Redpath made his way from one island of light to the next. The renewal of the pity she had felt earlier was like a physical pain to Leila. She watched Redpath's diminishing figure until it was lost in the tunnel of perspective, then she drove across the road and parked outside the flats.

On reaching the first landing she discovered he had left the door open and the lights switched on inside her apartment. She locked the door behind her, went straight to the telephone and dialled Nevison's number. The phone was answered immediately and she had begun to speak before realising it was a recording machine at the other end of the line. After stating her name and requesting a return call without delay, she hung up and stood by the phone for another minute, unsuccessfully trying to think of someone else to whom she might turn for help. Frank Pardey was unlikely to be in at that time, and even had he been she could not face the prospect of telling him that John was temporarily insane and had thrown her out of her own flat and stolen her television set, but that no charges were to be preferred.

Feeling tense and nervous, she slipped out of her coat and hung it up, and for the sake of the physical action tidied away the remains of the evening meal and washed the dishes. A profound sadness had settled over her by the time she finished, colouring all her thoughts and threatening to overwhelm her each time she considered the extent of the calamity which had overtaken Redpath. In only two days he had been transformed from an unremarkable, likeable *flâneur* with a certain desperate charm, whose main fault had been possessiveness, into an unpredictable stranger with a mind which appeared to have been sapped by the wildest outpourings of the super-nature cultists and flying saucer cranks.

One of the most disturbing aspects of the change was the air of utter, fanatical conviction with which he elaborated his fantasies. Leila had known a boy in Pangbourne who had drifted into a mental never-never land and who on occasion had talked

136

for hours about the emissaries from the Kingdom of Orion who would descend from the skies some day and seek him out, but always there had been a lurking bafflement in his eyes. The reason for it was that he had retained some contact with reality and was struggling to reconcile two conflicting world-views. John, on the other hand, spoke with a dreadful certainty, was entirely *convinced*. She knew little about abnormal psychology, but she had a growing suspicion that delusions of such completeness and intensity were likely to have a lasting effect. Could it be that Compound 183 was not merely psychosomimetic, but had served as a trigger for permanent mental derangement?

The idea that the old John Redpath might be gone for ever brought with it the realization that she had unconsciously begun to accept him as a fixture in her life. Ruffled by the discovery that the part of her which romantic writers referred to as the heart—and which she had presumed to keep fully under control—was in fact a wilful organ, capable of hatching subversive schemes of its own, Leila made some coffee and retired to the living-room to await Nevison's call. At midnight she thought of going to bed, but decided against it on the off-chance that what she had to say to Nevison might prompt him to come to the flat. She made herself comfortable on the settee, read the first two chapters of a paperback novel without getting into the story, and eventually relaxed into a light sleep.

The measured clamour of the phone bell shocked her into wakefulness at a few minutes past one. She sat up, feeling cold and apprehensive, ran into the hall and picked up the phone.

"Thank you, thank you for ringing, Henry," she said. "I've been waiting for . . ."

"Pardon me." The interruption came from an unfamiliar voice. "Am I calling the right number for Mr Redpath?"

Leila identified the accent as American and her sense of foreboding suddenly increased. "You've got the right number, but John isn't at home at the moment."

"Oh! When will he be available?"

"Not for some time," she said, then yielded to an impulse she scarcely understood. "He was called away on an urgent matter, but he asked me to take your call. I'm Leila Mostyn and I work with John at the institute. I know why he telephoned you, of course."

"I was really hoping to speak to Mr Redpath."

"Isn't that Mr Knight of the *Gilpinston Bugle*?"

"Yes, indeed." Apparently reassured by the foreknowledge of his name, Knight allowed a note of animation to enter his voice. "I've been down to 13th Avenue, Miss . . . Mizz . . ."

"Leila, please."

"Thank you, Leila. As I was saying, I've been to the house—and it's all there! Every detail checks out as predicted—even the name of the owners. A Mr and Mrs T. E. Rodgers, I'm told, though nobody in the street has seen them around for quite some time. I thought Mr Redpath would want to know right off."

"It was good of you to call," Leila said numbly. She floundered for a moment, unable to make the orthodox logical connections which would prove that this, too, was spurious evidence, that no assessments of John Redpath needed to be revised.

"I'd like to get the story into tomorrow's paper, but Mr Redpath didn't give me a number for . . . umm . . . Professor Nevison," Knight continued. "Do you happen to . . ?"

"Professor Nevison is out of town," Leila said quickly, almost as a reflex. "I should warn you that he's very sceptical about the whole thing. To be perfectly honest, he'll be pretty annoyed when he learns that John spoke to you without his authorization. He takes the view that every bit of that information could have been obtained from directories or letters or from conversation."

"I thought so, too—except for the bit about the bathroom."

"The bathroom?" Leila was suddenly aware of the darkness which pressed inwards at all the windows. "What about the bathroom?"

"Well, it turns out they had quite a bit of excitement in that neighbourhood yesterday morning. The house has been empty for a while, but one of the local kids noticed the front door lying open and he decided to have a walk inside. Probably hoping to pick up some small change—you know how it is with kids. Anyway, he came out of there an awful lot faster than he went in, and his mother found him hiding under his bed. It took her about an hour to get him to talk about it, but the kid swore he went up to the bathroom—just to use the facilities, you understand—and he saw two corpses lying in the tub."

"How ghastly," Leila said in a distant voice.

"That's not all of it. The kid said the bodies had no skin on them, and apparently he got so worked up that his mother sent for the police. When they got there the house was all closed up, but a woman who lives across the street said she'd seen a red-headed guy in a brown jacket running into it earlier on. So the cops got a locksmith to let them in and they checked the bathroom."

"Well?"

"It was as clean as a whistle. Nothing there. The whole place was empty."

Leila made her voice cool, unimpressed. "In other words, the whole episode amounts to precisely nothing."

"You don't understand," Knight whinnied. "Mr Redpath told me there was something . . ."

"Mr Redpath has a vivid imagination—and I really don't think there's any point in continuing this conversation. Good-bye, Mr Knight." Leila hung up the phone on the reporter's startled protests and slumped back against the wall, breathing deeply, bracing herself as though the world was tilting away from under her feet.

She remained in that attitude for more than a minute, then straightened up and walked to her coat, which was hanging on the opposite wall. The gilded black booklet of her passport was partially visible in one of the pockets. She stared at it with sombre eyes, coming to a decision, then went into the bedroom and began to pack an overnight bag.

PART THREE

Grand mal

CHAPTER 9

THE NIGHT HAD passed like an episode from one of his dreams.

Having rushed Leila off in the direction of London, he had thought about spending the night in her flat, but had decided against it on the grounds that a chance call or visit from almost anybody could lead to awkwardness. He had then set out to walk to his own place on Disley High Street, then had come the realisation that the wound in his midriff was still bleeding copiously and looked like continuing to do so. As far as he, the essential John Redpath, had been concerned it was nothing more than a minor irritation—he could have endured the pain and the sopping coldness of his clothing almost indefinitely—but another voice had warned him that he needed to preserve his strength and resources for a contest that lay ahead.

He had detoured to the casualty department of Calbridge General Hospital, where his arrival—soon after the closing time of the town's bars—had created the impression that he had been injured in a brawl. Only his patent sobriety and a display of jocular respectability had persuaded the young doctor to forget about the police and accept his story about an accident with a woodworking chisel. He had been cleaned, stitched, dusted with powders, bandaged, injected against tetanus, lectured, issued with a treatment card and sent home in an ambulance. In the blessed neutral tranquillity of his own apartment he had crawled into a cool bed and, against all the odds, had slept soundly until dawn.

Wakening to a world of grey light, with the ghosts of sensory impressions beginning to crowd in on him from all over the building, he knew at once that the E.S.P.-enhancing effects of Compound 183 had not yet diminished.

He also knew that on the previous night he had unwittingly, through exhaustion and cerebral overloading, hit on the best tactic for coping with his present situation. The trick was to avoid thinking graphically about his plans, to move like an automaton, to exist like a zombie. The thing in the cellar in Raby Street, the Once-born, was still linked to him in some way—as had been proved by the awesome moment of triple existence, with all its revelations—but the contact would never be as complete as the alien would wish because the necessary interfaces could not exist between minds that were so dissimilar.

Rapport was the word for the missing element, he decided. There was a kind of communication on some levels, but no rapport, and as long as that was the case he could continue to be himself, to think with one part of his brain and let his actions be guided by another. Always presuming that he retained control over his actions . . .

The family wants me back. They might be out looking for me! What the hell could I do if Albert appeared right here in the room?

How much time is left, anyway? How much time before the megadeaths come?

Galvanised by the urgency which had haunted him the night before, Redpath rolled sideways from under the sheets. He froze as he felt the pain from the knife wound returning with something like its original intensity. Moving more cautiously, he stood up nursing his side and got dressed in a lightweight polo-neck sweater and a fresh pair of slacks. It was rapidly growing brighter outside and the clatter of a milk float in the distance told him the town was coming to life. He took his simulated-leather hold-all from a cupboard, dropped five handkerchiefs—all he had—into it and closed the zip. Without taking time to eat or shave, he picked up the hold-all and Leila's television set—it wouldn't be too heavy to carry, he felt—and let himself out of the apartment.

The small section of the district he could see from the corridor windows looked indomitably normal, as always. The plane trees, the cindery car park, the builder's yard with its stacks of concrete lamp standards, the semi-detached houses and assorted garages—

all seemed to project the same message, that *this* was the real universe, secure and unchanging, and that to think otherwise was insanity. Redpath averted his eyes, hurried to the central stairway and went down to the street. Traffic was sparse at that hour—consisting of little more than a few steelworks employees heading in the direction of the plant by cycle and car—and he felt unusually conspicuous carrying a television set.

He turned into a sidestreet as quickly as possible, and that was the beginning of a day of drifting, loitering and trying to merge into his surroundings.

At mid-morning he bought a gallon of two-star petrol at a garage which charged him a twenty-pence deposit on the loan of a dented can which had once held engine oil. A little later he bought a disposable cigarette lighter and four large bottles of lemonade. Short of money and now too heavily loaded to keep on the move, he opted for spending the rest of the day in a public park. Churchill Gardens was the nearest, but if Betty York and the others were looking for him that was one of the places they were likely to try, and he had no wish to meet any of them until he was ready.

He walked to a smaller park which was favoured by pensioners largely because it did not incorporate a children's playground. The day was warm and pleasant, well suited for sun-bathing, and when he had established himself with his possessions at the centre of a grassy area he felt reasonably certain of attracting no undue attention from passers-by, police included. He took off his jacket and sweater, and rested for a while to ease the throbbing in the region of his stomach, then sipped some of the lemonade. His thirst quenched, he surreptitiously emptied the four bottles into the grass and filled them with petrol from the can. He replaced the stoppers and put the bottles back into the hold-all, wrapping them in the handkerchiefs which were later to serve as fuses.

That done, his modest arsenal assembled, he lay down and tried to blank out his mind—a task which proved exceptionally difficult.

The blue lens of the sky looked exactly as it had always done, but now he was acutely aware of the fact that it was a window into space, a window through which other eyes could peer down-

145

wards. His brief communion with the alien hunter had let him know it was close to the Earth, but how close was close? And was there a possibility that, even as he lay there, those ethereal blue arches could become the scene of the first interstellar battle in human history? The hunter, the thing which thought of itself as the Thrice-born, seemed to have a total disregard for life forms other than its own, and it might therefore be surprised to find orbital defences screening its quarry. Redpath doubted if laser-armed killer satellites—if such things existed—would be effective against a starship, but if the vessel came within range of nuclear warheads events might take an unexpected turn, unless it was able to make itself invisible to radar, perhaps by absorbing all incident radiation.

Too many unknown factors to evaluate—and I don't even read Aviation Week. And I'm thinking about things I wasn't going to think about . . .

Late in the afternon he saw a jetliner climbing high into the west, sowing a thin line of ice crystals across the sky, and he wondered how Leila was faring. It occurred to him, belatedly, that he should have arranged for her to telephone him somewhere and report on her progress. As it was, he would have to go ahead on schedule with his half of the operation and trust she had been given enough time to reach Gilpinston and . . .

I'm doing it again! Make out a list—ten film stars whose names began with the letter A. Bud Abbott. They don't need to be stars—John Abbott. John Agar. Brian Aherne. Woody Allen . . .

Soon after six o'clock the air cooled noticeably and a bright-rimmed canopy of cloud advanced from the direction of the Pennines, heralding an overdue break in the weather. Redpath donned his sweater and jacket, and delayed quitting the park for a further hour. While preparing to leave he made the cheering discovery that he had enough money in hand to buy a cup of tea. He walked slowly in the direction of the town centre, with an unseasonal leaden darkness gathering on the horizon behind him, and bought tea in an otherwise deserted café. The brew was too strong and too sweet, and he nostalgically savoured everything that was wrong with it.

By the time he reached the Woodstock Road the first drops

of rain were dappling the pavement, filling the air with the smell of dust. The children who used the streets in the district as a playground were rapidly moving indoors, possibly grateful for the weather change which was forcing a return to neglected pursuits which would be their mainstays through the winter. When Redpath left the main road and began cutting through sidestreets he saw warm glimmers of coloured light behind many of the windows and he knew that fires were being lit, television and radio sets switched on, kettles brought to the boil. The people were doing one of the things they did best, obeying racial memories, withdrawing into the cosy fug at the back of the cave. It was a good night for closing the curtains, wheeling the armchairs round to the fire and sitting with the rest of one's family, perhaps chatting, perhaps singing . . .

There's something wrong here. I should be afraid, but I'm not. Can it be that I'm actually looking forward to being one of the family again?

There was a slithering behind Redpath's forehead.

If its control grows stronger the closer I get, if it's an inverse square thing, how am I going to . . ?

He turned the corner into Raby Street and, laden with his hold-all in one hand and the television set in the other, trudged its length to number 131 like a son of the house returning from a harrowing day at work. Large drops of rain were pipping like airgun pellets into the accumulation of paper scraps in the front garden, scoring diagonal beaded lines on the dusty windows, encrusting the green moss caterpillars with liquid jewels. The curtains were drawn across the bay window of the front room, but Redpath knew the house was alive again. There was a coiling and uncoiling in his head. He walked up the short red-tiled path to the door, but as he was about to set his bag down the door was opened by Wilbur Tennent, who was sleek and splendid in a dove-grey checked suit. Betty York was visible beyond him, standing at the entrance to the living-room, still wearing her crimson T-shirt, low-waisted denims and sandals.

"Nice to see you, John boy." Tennent ushered Redpath into the hall amid eddies of cologne and after-shave, and turned back to Betty. "I told you he was coming home again."

She came forward, smiling with plum-coloured lips. "I see

147

you've brought your things, love. Let me give you a hand with them."

"I can manage," Redpath said, tightening his grip on the hold-all. "I'll just put this stuff up in my room, if you don't mind."

"You do that, then come down to the parlour—I'll be making the supper soon."

"Nice little television," Tennent commented. "John and me can watch the races on that."

"Leave him alone." Betty pushed Tennent into the front room, opening a way for Redpath to reach the stairs. As he was passing the doorway he glanced into the room and saw that all its furniture had been put back in position. Miss Connie and Albert were in their accustomed places. They were gazing at the glowing rectangular element of the gas fire, and neither showed any awareness of his arrival.

"I'll be down in a minute," he told Betty. "Just these things to get rid of."

"All right, love." She went into the room and closed the door, leaving him alone in the hall.

Redpath carried his bag and the television set up to the shadowy top of the house, past all the watchful doorways, and entered the room to which Betty York had shown him on his first visit. Everything was exactly as he remembered it, right down to the brown-ruled pink oilcloth on the floor. He put the television down on a tallboy, set his bag on a chair, opened it and stared for a moment at its contents, frowning.

Four bottles of . . . petrol. Dangerous stuff that. Perhaps I should warn Betty, ask her to get rid of it. Don't want to risk a fire. Especially not here, where I'm safe. Listerine Leila deserved everything I gave her, but the police won't see it that way. When they find her body they'll start hunting for me, but I'll be all right here. I'm safe here . . . with my family.

An unexpected giddiness touched Redpath, causing him to shuffle slightly to retain his balance. He palmed his eyes, pressing inwards on them to assuage a pain that was not quite a pain, and for an instant he glimpsed a montage of conflicting images. There was Leila's slim, tapering back—naked and disfigured with stab wounds; there was another image—comforting and disturbing at the same time—of Leila holding a black booklet which looked like a passport; and overlying everything was a transparent checkerwork of coloured panels in which lights flashed briefly and died, creating intricate, urgent designs which danced across his vision with the speed of wind patterns skimming a field of grain. There was a sense of imminence, of terrible danger, but the feeling passed as quickly as it had come. He lowered his hands, looked around the room, nodded in satisfaction, and walked down the dark stairway to where the others were waiting for him.

I'm all right here, he thought. *I'm safe here with my family.*

CHAPTER 10

A DAY OF waiting and worrying in the international building at
Heathrow Airport had left Leila Mostyn feeling more tired than
she would have thought possible.

There was a superabundance of passengers bound for the
United States, many of them youngsters who gave the impression
of having decided to go on the spur of the moment, and the
trade in stand-by tickets had been brisk. She had failed to get a
seat on a morning plane to Chicago, and had turned down some
indirect possibilities in favour of an extra 747 flight which had
been laid on to depart at noon. The difference in time zones
meant that it would have got her into Chicago's O'Hare field at
around three in the afternoon, local time, leaving her with a
reasonable four hours in which to reach Gilpinston. It would
have been better to have a greater margin, especially as she knew
that getting through the U.S. immigration checks could be a
time-consuming process, but at that stage she still felt she could
cope with the situation. There was, she had felt, enough time.

Then things had begun to awry.

First had come the announcement that a fault in the traffic
control radar at Frankfurt was going to delay the arrival of her
aircraft at Heathrow by two hours. Leila had been dismayed to
find her reserves of time cut in half at a stroke, but by then it
had become too late even to consider an indirect flight, and she
had settled down with a taut, fluttery feeling in her stomach to
adapt her thinking to a new and much more pressing schedule.
She had eaten a light meal in the snack bar and was trying to
relax afterwards with a glass of vermouth when a delay of a
further hour was announced, wringing an ironic cheer from some
of her fellow passengers.

It had been almost three o'clock before they had been able to

150

board the aircraft, and by that time she had entered a state of sick, nerve-thrumming anxiety. A bespectacled man in the next seat had tried to strike up a conversation with her, but on receiving her tight-lipped, abstracted replies had turned his attention to a magazine. A few minutes later the captain of the 747 had come on the address system and, with evident embarrassment, had explained that the late arrival at Heathrow had caused problems with the fuelling service and that there would be a wait of forty-five minutes before the aircraft would be tanked up and ready to go. The news had roused a further cheer and, through some kind of reverse psychology, had strengthened the holiday spirit among the younger passengers, some of whom left their seats and stood in the aisles loudly swapping witticisms with their friends.

Leila had withdrawn into a bubble of loneliness, separating herself from an environment which was rapidly beginning to seem meaningless and hostile, a daunting mélange of shouts and bellowing laughs, unfamiliar sights and smells, pneumatic hisses and hydraulic whines. It was a world of normal people doing normal things, and she was no part of it. She had been afraid to think too much about what she was doing, and right up to the moment when the heavy doors had been pulled into place, sealing the fuselage, she had been plagued by urges to leave her seat and quit the aircraft. Only when the engines had been started, sending expectant tremors through the floor and the arms of her seat, did she allow the mental floodgates to burst apart.

What have you done to me, John? The things I took to be evidence last night, when I was thrown completely off balance, aren't evidence at all. A scrap of newspaper with the wrong date, a couple of odd coincidences . . .

My God, what am I doing to myself? Putting myself in jail, that's all! I'm planning to go to the United States and burn down a house with Molotov cocktails. They'll lock me up and throw away the key!

Leila was staring straight ahead at two male members of the cabin staff who were struggling to fit a large aluminium container for hot meals into its closet-like storage compartment. So great was the turmoil in her mind that perhaps ten minutes had gone by without any progress being made before she realized that the saga of hitches and delays for that particular flight had not yet ended. The alloy meal container was still blocking an aisle and the aircraft had not yet moved away from the embarkation bay.

A stewardess tried to give the two men some advice and was sent away, pink-cheeked and angry. The men renewed their efforts to stow the container, now making a considerable noise as they hit it with fists and shoulders, and a minute later were joined by a senior steward and a member of the flight crew. A whispered argument developed, during which Leila's sensitively attuned ears picked up the words "engineer" and "unseal". Her heart began a slow, steady pounding.

The captain's eventual announcement that there was to be yet another delay brought a round of derisory applause which Leila scarcely heard. She undid her seat belt, stood up and took her coat and bag from the overhead locker, and was walking up the aisle within seconds of the mid-fuselage door being opened. A tall steward in a half-sleeved white shirt stepped in front of her as she tried to squeeze out past a mechanic who was entering with a box of tools.

"Sorry, miss," the steward said. "You can't go through there. Is there something wrong?"

"I've changed my mind about flying today." She made her voice firm and self-possessed. "I want to leave the aircraft, and I believe I'm entitled to do so."

The steward shook his head. "Passengers aren't permitted to disembark after the luggage has been put on board. It's a security regulation, miss."

"I don't care about your regulations."

"If you would care to return to your seat I'm sure we can . . ."

"I don't care to return to my seat because this aircraft was supposed to take off more than four hours ago, and I've missed an important appointment because of the delay, and now there's no point in my going to the States—so I'm not going." Leila increased the level of her voice, attracting the attention of passengers in the nearer part of the cabin. "If you try to keep me on board against my will, while your so-called engineers try to load the sandwich box, I promise you I'll kick up the loudest, longest and nastiest fuss you've ever heard."

"You don't understand, miss," the steward said unhappily.

"If you were to leave now we'd have to unload all the luggage and . . ."

"*You* are the one who doesn't understand," Leila countered. "If I'm obstructed from leaving at once I'll go to the newspapers at the very first opportunity and I'll tell them there was a four-hour delay over the packed lunches on this flight. I'll make sure that everybody in the country hears about the kind of service this airline offers."

The steward spread his hands. "Please wait here—I'll let you speak to Captain Sinclair."

The ensuing thirty minutes were among the most difficult and embarrassing of Leila's entire life, especially as her abrupt change of mind about flying had aroused the suspicions of the customs, immigration and security staffs, but she weathered the period with an icy composure which did not crack until she had driven out of the airport grounds and was travelling north in the vicinity of Uxbridge. She pulled in to the side of the road as tears blurred out her vision, and sat with her forehead resting on the upper rim of the steering wheel.

"I'm sorry, John," she whispered. "I'm so sorry. I did try, in spite of what you'll think—but tonight you're on your own."

CHAPTER 11

THE FAMILY WAS united again, all its members sitting in a semi-circle in the downstairs front room.

Betty York sat nearest the wall on the left of the fireplace, with flecks of red lacquer on her toenails and nacreous brown lacquer on her fingernails. Next to her was Redpath, and then came Wilbur Tennent, plump and handsome, sitting upright and leaning forward slightly in an attitude which might have been designed to prevent his lustrous suit from creasing. Beside him was Albert, nodding and sniffing, massive hands interlaced across his stomach, clad as always in his brown boiler suit and scuffed work boots. And closest to the wall on the right of the fireplace was Miss Connie, with ivory-coloured hair and ribboned glasses, her angular but broad-shouldered figure draped in a grey cardigan and ankle-length black dress. She was knitting industriously, adding another irregular section to the dimly seen mass in the corner behind her.

"Before I forget, John." Tennent reached into his pocket, took out a thin bundle of banknotes which were secured by an elastic band, and dropped them into Redpath's lap. "We connected with Parsnip Bridge, just like I told you."

"Thanks," Redpath said, belatedly realising he had no idea of what had happened to the previous winnings he had received in a like manner. He wondered briefly if Tennent had managed to take the money back again without his noticing, or if for some reason Miss Connie had spirited it away from him.

Tennent rubbed his hands, boyishly gleeful. "We're going well, John boy. I've got a double lined up for us tomorrow, and if you'll take my advice you'll put . . ."

"Leave him alone," Betty cut in. "I've told you before that John isn't interested in your get-rich-quick schemes."

154

"Why shouldn't he be? Everybody likes a bit of extra loot. Isn't that right?" Tennent turned to Redpath for support, showing his small regular teeth in a companionable grin. He gazed at Redpath for a few seconds, his look of pleasure slowly fading, and a hint of perplexity came into his eyes. "John? You like it here, don't you? I mean, you wouldn't do anything to . . ."

"Leave him be," Betty snapped. "How can he rest with you going on at him the whole time?"

Tennent subsided into his chair in silence, shooting Redpath an occasional thoughtful glance. Redpath, feeling oddly relieved, set the bundle of money in a neutral position on the arm of his chair. There followed a long period during which nobody spoke, but in which the room was full of small sounds—the popping and muttering of the gas fire, the ticking of the clock, the clicking of Miss Connie's needles, odd little snuffles and snorts from Albert. The curtains breathed steadily in the bay window. Redpath allowed his gaze to roam the walls and it came to rest centred on something small and dark that was clinging to the wallpaper. It was a crane-fly, possibly the same one he had noticed two nights earlier, seemingly still in the same place, still vibrating to the same mindless rhythm.

Oh Christ, what makes them do that? I thought it would have been dead by this time. How long can a daddy-long-legs go on living, anyway? A frog can live for forty years. Just think of it! It'd be bad enough being a frog for one year—but to have to keep it up for forty years! Leila, how can you be dead if you . . ?

"I know what we need," Betty York said, getting to her feet. "A nice cup of tea and something to eat."

That's not what I need. I need to drink some water, a hell of a lot of water, and to watch some television.

"The sandwiches are ready, love, and the tea won't be long," Betty said to Redpath as she crossed the semi-circle of chairs in front of him, momentarily filling his field of view with long black hair, taut blue haunches and copper rivets. "You like Plumrose, don't you?"

Redpath nodded, thinking bemusedly about his sudden thirst for water and the urge to watch television. *Jack Haley isn't on tonight, is he? I saw him last night—but who was I with?*

Betty returned in a surprisingly short time and Tennent moved

155

his chair to let her wheel the laden trolley into the centre of the group. She poured five cups of tea from a huge glazed pot. Miss Connie set her knitting aside, took a sandwich and began to eat with a zest which seemed inappropriate for her age and meagre build. The sight of the thick-cut, pink-tongued layers of bread brought it home to Redpath that he had had no food all day.

He put four sandwiches on a plate and was biting into the last of them when he realised that Albert, two seats away on his right, had not taken anything to eat or drink. Mildly curious, he leaned forward to see past Tennent and observed that Albert had not changed his position in anyway since he had entered the room. The little man was sprawled in the chair with his legs extended and his hands still clasped across his middle. His enormous chin was jutting more than ever, his eyes were staring straight ahead—opaque as those of a hospital patient under the heaviest sedation—and almost continual tremors coursed through his limbs. Lentils of perspiration dotted his brow.

The other members of the group, seemingly oblivious to what was happening, continued to eat in silent concentration.

Redpath set his plate down, frowning, and twisted in his seat to be able to see Albert more clearly. The inarticulate sounds Albert had been making grew louder and his eyes turned in Redpath's direction—pained, pleading, desperate. They seemed to hold a message for Redpath, to be trying to remind him of some terrible responsibility he had once undertaken. He began to feel afraid.

"Isn't this nice?" Miss Connie said in her scratchy voice, smiling, showing her antique dentures.

"Very nice," Tennent and Betty said in unison.

Redpath turned away from Albert, looked at the clock above the fireplace and saw that its filigreed hands stood at almost ten-thirty. Far in the back of his mind there was an uneasy flickering, a sense of time going by too quickly. He picked up his partly-eaten sandwich, found he no longer wanted it and settled back into his chair. His thoughts began to wander and, for some reason he was at a loss to understand, he became acutely conscious of the house, not as a conceptual unity, but as an assemblage of various architectural elements. The room was still a room, but he also saw it was a roughly cubical volume of

156

space, artificially contrived and bounded. Instinctively he tended to equate a floor with solid ground, but the solid-seeming floor of the room he was in was in fact a kind of platform or bridge. It was a structural sandwich consisting of an upper layer of boards, a central filling of timber joists, a bottom layer of laths and plaster, and beneath that . . . beneath that was the cellar of the house . . . a kingdom of darkness that began only inches below his feet . . . and there was something . . .

He blinked, taken aback, as he discovered that Tennent had turned in his direction and was pointing at him with an expression of twinkling exuberance on his plump-cheeked face.

"Keeee . . . pright on to the end of the road," Tennent chanted, "keeee . . . pright on to the end."

"That's the spirit," Betty said, joining in the song.

Redpath glanced at Miss Connie, who nodded encouragingly, and he heard himself begin to sing in a low, tentative voice. The members of the family had begun to enjoy themselves, like any other group of normal people in Calbridge, and if Albert had no wish to join in that was his own affair.

Some time later Redpath noticed the clock again, and was obscurely jolted to realise that there were only fifteen minutes to midnight. Again there was a curious shifting and slithering behind his eyes.

I know what's happening to Albert, he thought, making an intuitive-cum-telepathic leap. *He's putting up a fight. He's fighting my battle. He knows that time is running out, and he's trying to help me—but what are we fighting?*

Redpath rose slowly to his feet and addressed Betty with a frozen smile. "The bathroom's just at the head of the stairs, isn't it?"

"That's right, love." She eyed him soberly. "Don't be too long."

"I won't." He left the room and went out into the pitch darkness of the hall. It took him some time to locate a light switch and when he depressed it a small fitment glowed in the high ceiling, emitting a weak radiance the colour of moths' wings. The kitchen door was visible a short distance away as a rectangle of sentient blackness. He turned away from it, went up the stairs and into the bathroom, pulled the cord of the

157

ceiling switch and tried to bolt the door behind him. The paint-clogged shoot-bolt was so badly aligned with its keeper that he was unable to drive it home.

Abandoning the attempt, he went to the washbasin, turned on the cold tap and stooped to put his mouth under it. The water jetted out faster than he had expected, taking his breath away, but he swallowed it and kept on swallowing. Within seconds his stomach felt tight and swollen. He raised his head to snatch some air, almost gagged, and began to drink again.

Do you know, he could almost hear Dr Hyall's voice, *that in the darker days of medicine one of the standard tests to determine if a person had epilepsy was to give him a few pints of water to drink?*

A sudden spasm of nausea forced Redpath to straighten up. He gripped the rim of the basin with both hands, fighting to control the upward thrusts of his diaphragm, and knew there was less than no point in trying to go on, that taking another mouthful of water would result in a violent spewing of all that was in his stomach. It was time to watch some television.

And be careful when you're near a faulty television set, Dr Hyall was saying, smiling benignly at him through a tunnel into another time. *If something needs adjusting, specially the vertical hold—let somebody else do it. Never kneel in front of a TV set that has a rolling picture.*

He opened the bathroom door, went out onto the landing and turned towards the front of the house. The main part of the landing and the stair to the upper floor were on his right; the stair leading back down to the hall was on his left. He was veering to the right when the living room door opened down below and Betty York came out into the hall. She was joined at once by Tennent and Miss Connie. All three eyed him intently.

"Are you all right, love?" Betty said.

"Couldn't be . . . better," Redpath replied, fighting to put words together, to think and not to think. "Jack Haley . . . television."

He gestured in the general direction of his room and went towards the upper stair. There was the sound of footsteps on the stair below him. He quickened his pace, reached the top landing and stumbled through the dimness into his room. Closing the door and turning on the light in one movement, he saw that the lock was of the type that incorporated a small brass bolt. He stared blankly at the bolt for several seconds, then thumbed it into place just as somebody tried the handle.

"What are you doing in there, John boy?" Tennent pleaded. "Open the door."

" You don't understand," Redpath mumbled. "Jack Haley . . . television." He removed the television set from the bed, carried it across the room and knelt at a power point in the skirting board.

"Come on, John, you don't know what you're missing," Tennent said in a wheedling voice and began to sing. " Keeee . . . pright on to the end of the road . . ." The words of the song were lost in a violent pounding on the door, a sound which could only have been produced by two or more pairs of fists beating on it at the same time. Women's voices joined in the din.

Redpath shook his head, panic-stricken. " Favourite film. They don't make them like that any . . ." He tried to ram the connector at the end of the television's power lead into the socket, but the two components refused to mate. He tried twice more before realising what was wrong. The connector had modern rectangular pins and the socket was of the old-fashioned round-pin type.

"They don't make them like that any more," he repeated dully, staring at the useless plug.

The hammering on the door behind him ceased and was replaced by a measured and powerful thudding which signalled that Tennent was trying to break it open with his shoulder. Redpath glanced back and saw that the wooden jamb was curving inwards with every blow. The three on the landing no longer sounded like human beings, and at least one of them was making strange, wet, sucking noises.

"Slughhh, slughhh, slughhh."

His face crumpling with despair, Redpath wrenched the connector from the end of the television flex, exposing the bare wires. He spread the wires with his fingers and crammed them into the holes of the socket, heedless of his skin touching metal. There was a sputtering crackle, a spiky blaze of purple, and he was hurled backwards into a gloating and greedy blackness.

CHAPTER 12

SADNESS PERVADED THE enormous composite entity that was the ship, sadness over the preparations for death.

The emotion had nothing to do with the knowledge that a member of the First Race was soon to be dispersed—he was a renegade who had threatened the very foundations of his own society and there could be no place for him in an orderly continuum. Nor was there any concern that a considerable area of the seventh planet, counting inwards from the rim of the system, was to be rendered sterile. Its inhabitants belonged to that almost-universal class of beings, the simulacra. They did not possess the ability to commune with the Star-that-lives, and therefore could be regarded as accidental association of cells, pseudo-beings whose existence or annihilation was without relevance to the great scheme.

The sadness that affected the conglomerate entity of the ship was due to the fact that a part of its own structure would have to die, to be sacrificed in order to bring about the dispersal of the Once-born.

Remains of the outer portions of the fugitive ship had been detected through their lingering life-echoes, and the location pinpointed on an island close to one of the major land masses. A section of the living skin of the hunter ship had detached itself, painfully, from the main shell and had reformed in a shape suitable for high-speed atmospheric penetration. Within it, a portion of the ship's body matter had already undergone voluntary degeneration to the viral state. In that condition, on exposure to oxygen, it would rapidly eliminate all life forms over a wide area before reaching the inactive phase.

Those losses to the ship's corpus had been unwelcome enough, but the real tragedy was that a fragment of the Thrice-born, a

160

member of the First Race, had been required to separate from the parent body and make ready to die. Lacking many of the primitive psi-powers of a Once-born, the hunter was unable to deliver or even control the pod by psychokinesis. It was necessary for him to sacrifice a portion of his own being to drive and guide the living bomb which was to be the instrument of justice. And the sense of bereavement was all the more keenly felt because the death it was to experience would be final—under the circumstances there could be no ingestion, purification and renascence.

The duty had been assigned and the responsibility accepted many years earlier, however, and there was to be no turning back.

Gently, and without remorse, the pod moved away from the vast bulk of the ship and began the long descent to Earth.

CHAPTER 13

REDPATH AWOKE TO a silence that was both external and internal, a blessed sense of his own personal humanity. He felt sane and untainted, privileged simply to be alive. The feeling, the modest joy, sustained him for the space of a dozen heartbeats, then he looked at his watch and saw there were only six minutes to midnight.

Where has everybody gone? Was the door too much for them? Have they gone away, or are they on the landing waiting for me to come out?

He sat up and looked around the quiet bedroom, and at that moment a blizzard of memory fragments imploded upon him, clicking into place, reassembling a terrible picture in his mind. Time was running out! Leila would be outside the house in Gilpinston at that very minute; the megadeaths were coming; and he had an appointment with something that waited in the cellar.

He stood up, almost retched and fought to control the quivering weakness of his limbs. Anvil blows were ringing through his temples. He looked down at the stripped wire lying beside the power point and realised he had been lucky not to electrocute himself or perhaps precipitate a full-scale *grand mal* which could have stretched him on the floor for hours. As it was, he was unable to decide if he had suffered a very minor epilepsy or had simply been shocked into unconsciousness. The physical after-effects were ambiguous—but the vitally important result was that for the time being he was his own man again, released from outside control, free to act and think independently. And precious seconds were flittering away into eternity.

The hold-all was still sitting on the chair where he had left it. Redpath opened the bag, took out one of the four bottles it con-

162

tained and twisted the cap. It was moist with seeping petrol which combined with the sweat of his palms to reduce his grip, and the metal cap refused to turn. Swearing with impatience, he glanced at the bedroom door, grateful for the fact that it had been strong enough to resist Wilbur Tennent's efforts to burst it open. In that instant there was an appalling crash and an upper panel of the door was caved inwards by a massive metal object which revealed itself to be the head of a sledge-hammer.

Redpath stared at the door, momentarily paralysed, as the hammer was withdrawn from the gaping hole. Tennent's hand appeared in its place and began groping for the lock.

Acting without conscious thought, Redpath snatched a handkerchief from his bag and used it to improve his grip on the bottle cap. This time it turned immediately. He removed the cap and wadded the handkerchief into the neck of the bottle with his forefinger. Holding the improvised bomb in the crook of his left arm, he reached into the bag and took out another bottle. Again he had to struggle to remove the cap, and had barely suceeded when the bolt on the door emitted a sharp metallic *clack*.

Tennent opened the door and sidled into the room. He was carrying the big hammer at the ready and his eyes were those of a corpse.

With him came Betty York and Miss Connie, both of whom were holding hand-picks, the type of tool used by masons to chip out mortar, sharp-pointed and easily capable of penetrating a man's skull. One part of Redpath's mind, escaping into irrelevancy, noted that all three tools were brand-new and thought, *Good old Miss Connie—she always delivers the goods.*

"Stay back," he ordered, dry-mouthed, wondering if the three flesh-puppets before him could still be reached by human speech. "I don't want to hurt you. Do you understand what I'm saying?"

Miss Connie bulged her eyes at him and said, "Slughhh, slughhh, slughhh." And then, in spite of the fact that the bed was between her and Redpath, she came walking straight towards him, stepping up on to the mattress with unnatural litheness.

Tennent and Betty moved round the end of the bed. Redpath backed away, flailing the air with the opened bottle of petrol, hurling its contents across the room in wavering zigzags. The three paused for a moment as the volatile fluid splashed across their bodies, then resumed their advance. Tennent was shifting his grip on the sledge-hammer, preparing to commit murder with it, and the two women were making little clawing movements with their picks.

"I'm warning you," Redpath breathed, dropping the empty bottle and dragging the cigarette lighter out of his jacket pocket. Betty hissed and darted forward. Redpath flicked the wheel of the lighter and his whole hand caught fire, sheathing itself in a gauntlet of pale yellow flame. He pushed Betty away from him, simultaneously igniting her clothing, and she staggered against Tennent. Miss Connie came swooping down on Redpath from the direction of the bed, like a falling scarecrow, and he felt a stabbing pain in his left shoulder. He hit her with his burning fist, saw her topple sideways, and sprang across the bed towards the door. He reached it in a single leap and hurled himself out onto the landing, peripherally aware that Tennent had already stripped himself of his jacket and was using it to extinguish Betty's clothing. Miss Connie had bounded to her feet like a champion gymnast and was tearing at her black dress.

The comparatively cool petroleum flame which had enveloped Redpath's hand had blown away in the rush of air, leaving a stinging sensation. Fearful that the bedroom was about to explode, he ran to the stairs and plunged down them, still cradling his firebomb. He reached the middle landing, sprinted along it and was half-way down the stairs to the hall when he saw something that brought him to a slithering, bumping halt. The door to the living-room was open, creating a foreshortened dark aperture, and projecting from the bottom of that aperture he could see the toe of a workman's boot.

Albert's waiting for me! I could get by him all right, but there are all kinds of bolts on that front door, and while I'm trying to get them open he'll have lots of time to come up behind me. And with hands like his he doesn't even need a hammer or a pick-axe . . .

"Slughhh, slughhh," said a voice from above him, shockingly close, and a white-headed, skeletal figure, clad only in a silvery grey petticoat, lunged at him over the bannister of the landing. He warded off the clutching hands with a swing of his arm, heard footsteps thundering on the upper stairs, and launched himself to the bottom of the stairs in one dangerous bound. The newel post creaked as he swung round it and hurled himself towards the kitchen.

Nearly there, old son! Get the cellar door open, light the bottle and smash it on the steps, then sail out through that kitchen window. You've seen it in the flicks a hundred times, and if somebody like Randolph Scott can do it . . .

Redpath burst into the dark kitchen, turned to the right and pulled open the red door that led to the cellar. A greater darkness yawned at him from below, exhaling its warm breath. Ignoring the unmanning sense of dread that tried to buckle his knees, he raised the cigarette lighter and thumbed its rough-rimmed wheel. It failed to ignite. He tried again, aware of pounding footfalls in the hall, and again the flame was stillborn.

The valve! I forgot to hold down the frigging valve!

He thrust the lighter into the chilly wetness of the handkerchief-fuse and was in the act of spinning the wheel when somebody hit the kitchen door at speed from the other side. The door swatted Redpath on to the first of the cellar steps. He lost his footing and slid down several more steps in a sitting position. The bottle of petrol flew from his grasp and bounced down the steps into the blackness, with louder impacts each time.

Once, twice, thrice . . . silence.

It should have smashed! There's a concrete floor down there— so the bottle should have smashed!

An electric light came on, and in the same instant the sledgehammer whirred past Redpath's head and battered a huge cake of plaster out of the wall at his side. Wilbur Tennent—stripped to his vest and jockey shorts—was standing over him, glaring with his terrible corpse's eyes, already making another swing with the hammer. Redpath escaped him by leaping the rest of the way down into the cellar, and was committed to the descent, totally unable to turn back, when he saw that most of the walls and floor were covered with a shifting, glistening reddish-brown sludge. The mass, which was like a slurry of clotting blood and fragments of liver, was on the move. It was flowing away from the bottom of the steps, leaving a clear area at the centre of which lay Redpath's petrol bomb.

Dear God, my first nightmare was right!
I'VE WALKED INTO THE HOUSE'S STOMACH!

His capacity for terror exhausted, his mind saturated with dread, Redpath snatched up the bottle and backed into the corner nearest the bottom of the steps. The obscene tide ceased its retreat and began to flow towards him, reaching out with yearning stalks and tendrils which gorged and fattened on internal fluids before being reabsorbed into the main body.

At the same time Wilbur Tennent slowly came down the rest of the steps with his hammer, followed by Miss Connie and Betty York, who both were carrying their lethal little picks. Betty had pulled off her outer clothing, revealing the angry pinkness of burns on her stomach and thighs, and her hair was shrivelled into cindery lumps on one side of her head. Her eyes were like Tennent's, blobs of lifeless jelly.

Redpath, moving with the mechanical precision of a robot, thumbed the wheel of his lighter, this time remembering to hold down the gas valve. It produced a spear of blue flame which he touched to the bottle in his other hand, creating a flaming yellow torch which threw out light and heat. The edge of the creeping brown mucus immediately stopped moving. Redpath raised the bottle higher and by the extra illumination it provided saw that, far back in the amorphous mass, there was the suggestion of a central structure, a rounded hummock of protoplasm containing something which might have been a sunken eye. The sight of it began to draw the life from his body, threatening to turn him into an immobile assembly of levers and joints without volition of its own.

It's taking me again, Leila, and so quickly this time!

I've got to throw the bottle before it explodes in my face—but I've just realised why it won't work.

There's nothing down here to burn!

The petrol alone might injure the Once-born, but it's too big to be killed this way. I didn't expect it to be so big. It doesn't make any difference, anyway, because . . . because . . .

Even the capacity for thought deserted Redpath as he saw that Tennent had reached the bottom of the steps and was coming towards him with the hammer poised at his right shoulder. He tried to shift his weight in preparation for evasive action, but

166

a total paralysis had been imposed on his body. It was impossible for him even to open his fingers and drop the petrol bomb. Tennent moved closer, raised the hammer above his head and halted in that attitude, teetering, as the brown-clad figure of Albert materialized directly in front of him.

The appearance was instantaneous, magic, stupefying.

Although Redpath had deduced that the little man had the ability to teleport himself, actually seeing the power in action produced a pang of wonder which affected him significantly even though his perceptions were already overloaded by the imminence of death and the hideous encompassing presence of the alien creature. He stared in something like superstitious awe as Albert spread his arms, turning himself into a protective crucifix which stood between Redpath and the upraised hammer.

"Get out of the way," Tennent said in an inhuman monotone. "If you don't get out of the way I'll have to kill you."

"That would be a good idea," Albert replied softly, "but you can't do it. You see, I'm the only one here that the gaffer still needs. It's all happening, Wilbur—just the way Prince Reginald told us it were going to happen."

"He was lying."

"No! He told us the God's truth. It's been going on for ten minutes and more. The gaffer's been trying to make me take him to the other house. And I've been fighting him off, Wilbur. I've been *resisting*, Wilbur. For the first time in twelve years I got up enough spunk to resist the bugger."

The living brown walls of the cellar heaved once, like a chamber in a beating heart, and Albert staggered as though he had been struck. He turned to face Redpath. His face was pale, streaked by rivulets of sweat, and his eyes were flakes of ice.

"I owe this to you, lad. The gaffer's scared and he's getting old, so he can't keep me down like he's used to—but you gave him the most trouble. The harder he had to try to keep you down, the easier it was for me to come back up." Albert paused to swallow painfully. "You've got to keep fighting, lad. Don't pack up now. If you can throw that there bottle you're holding, that should do the trick. I can get us out of here . . . end this thing for good an' all."

Redpath was aware of the bottle becoming dangerously hot in

his hand, threatening to turn him into a human torch, but he was unable to hurl it away from himself. "I . . . I . . . Can you get me out, as well?"

Albert gave him a strange, sad smile. "You're not part of us yet, lad—you're still clean."

"Clean?"

"That's what I said. You see—you never had to help us feed the gaffer."

"Oh!" Redpath looked into Albert's eyes and saw something there that went far beyond ordinary pain, something he shrank from knowing.

"Aye, lad, it's as bad as that." Albert turned away to face Wilbur and the two women. "Don't leave it all to me and John! For pity's sake, give us a hand to get this thing over and done with at last." His voice was tortured, each word like the shattering of a bone.

Tennent opened his mouth, made a harsh rattling sound far back in his throat and swung the sledge-hammer. It slid from his grasp at the high point of its arc and went tumbling through the air to come down near the central mound of liver-like plasm. It disappeared below the surface in a dark welter of flying jelly.

A silent scream furled through Redpath's mind, drowning out his senses.

He was only distantly conscious of the loathsome brown tide surging forward, moving with appalling swiftness, reaching out with blind tentacles. It engulfed his own ankles and he felt pain there, but the sensation was numbed by his blurred awareness of what was happening to Tennent, Betty and Miss Connie. Where the slime touched the bare flesh of their legs the skin dissolved on the instant, leaving the musculature exposed and red, glistening with all the awful clarity of an anatomy chart. Miss Connie fell to her hands and knees in the slurry, then struggled up again with hands that seemed to be encased in crimson gloves.

Only Albert was untouched. He stood in a circle of clean concrete, unmoving, his eyes searing into Redpath's soul.

Redpath, humbled and inspired, made a supreme effort to throw the petrol bomb. His left arm gave a spastic jerk. The bottle slipped from his grasp and landed in the writhing brown ooze near his feet. It did not break, but there was an immediate spillage of burning petrol. The slurry retreated radially, like an iris springing open, and another soundless scream yammered through Redpath's head.

He clapped both hands to his temples and tried to focus his gaze on Albert. The little man had closed his eyes. His face, in spite of its acromegalic deformities, was that of an ancient high priest. Redpath had a final fragmentary vision of him—uniquely heroic in his scuffed boots and stained brown overalls with the pack of Lucky Strikes projecting from one pocket—then the image was blasted away in the incredible white heat of a furnace.

He existed no more.

The three capering crimson figures that had been with him existed no more.

The mass of sentient, brown protoplasm that had been with him existed no more.

Redpath *felt* the death of the Once-born. He sank to his knees in the pure, peaceful emptiness of the cellar and for an instant, with the last vestiges of the telepathic facility which had been foisted upon him, he experienced the surprise and satisfaction which coursed through the composite entity of the alien ship. He even picked up echoes of the smaller joy, faint as starlight in the noon-time sky, of the invisibly falling pod as it was recalled from the brink of non-existence.

Then the third eye of his mind closed for ever.

CHAPTER 14

THERE REMAINED A lingering sadness, an intense pity for four human beings whose lives had been blighted by something worse than any disease, who had lived in dreadful captivity, and whose deaths had come in a climax of pain and terror. And there must have been many others throughout the years—people like Prince Reginald and the Rodgers, the unfortunate owners of the house in Gilpinston. Who was to say how many flayed bodies of humans and animals and birds, perhaps still alive, had been spirited out of the cellar and disposed of by Albert or Miss Connie?

Redpath knelt for a time on the clean white concrete of the underground floor, wondering if he would ever again know a peaceful night of sleep, then it came to him that he, at least, was still alive—and was faced with all the practical responsibilities of the living.

He went through the silent house from top to bottom, turning out all the lights, making sure there were no smouldering scraps which might later create a full-scale blaze. His progress was slow—largely because the pain from his ankles and injured left shoulder had combined with that from the older wound at his stomach to impede or complicate his every move—and it was past one o'clock when he let himself out through the front entrance. He made certain that the lock on the outer door had engaged properly, then picked up his hold-all and the portable television set and went along the short, red-tiled path to the street.

The rain was still falling steadily, producing yellow candy floss haloes around the street lamps, and the windows were dark in every house. There was no sound except for the lapping of water in the cast-iron downpipes and gutters. *It's beautiful*, he thought, gazing about him in deep contentment. *If my hair was black, and if I had bullet holes in me instead of odd punctures, this could be a great old Francis Lederer movie.*

He squared his shoulders and, without a further glance at number 131, set off in the direction of the blue-green aerial glow which marked the course of the Woodstock Road. Before he had taken a dozen paces the wetness of the pavement had penetrated what remained of his shoes, but he was in a mood to enjoy any kind of natural sensation, and he continued walking steadily, undismayed.

On reaching the first corner he turned right and was angling across the street when a cherry-coloured mini came into view a short distance ahead. His immediate recognition of the vehicle had nothing to do with any kind of prescience. Blinking with gratitude, he stopped under a street lamp and waited until the car had drawn to a halt beside him. When Leila opened the near-side door he raised the television set as a signal for her to lower the back of the passenger seat, then stowed it with his bag on the rear seat, all without speaking. He maintained his silence while he got in, sat down and closed the door.

"Just tell me one thing," he said, after what seemed a suitable pause, "did you bring me a stick of Chicago rock?"

"Oh, *John*!" She blurted his name with a mixture of evident concern and relief. "I've been so worried about you. Last night you were so . . ."

"I know what I was like last night, but I promise you I won't be like that ever again. It's all over."

"I did try to go to the States," she said quietly, huddling into her coat. "But I ran out of nerve."

He shook his head. "No—you ran out of conviction. You couldn't really believe any of it, could you?"

"I'm sorry, John."

"It isn't your fault." He smiled his reassurance. "I want you to do me a couple of favours, though. The first one is that I want you to listen to me while I go over the whole thing right from the start. There's nobody else I could talk to about this, and I need to spell it all out just once, just to get it clear in my head, just to separate the nightmares from the reality before I bury the whole episode. Is that all right?"

171

"I'm listening." She returned his smile, put her hand on his shoulder and quickly withdrew it as he flinched away. "What's the matter, John?"

"That reminds me of the second favour I was going to ask—would you please drive me to the hospital?"

"What have you done to yourself?"

"What have I . . ?" The simple, natural question—with its implication that, in the absence of any proof to the contrary, his various injuries had to have prosaic causes—gave Redpath a sudden clear insight into how his story was going to sound.

This hole in my shoulder? Why, quaint old Miss Connie did that with a pick just before I set fire to her.

This burn on my hand? Oh, I got that because the Once-born paralysed me and made me hold a blazing petrol bomb a bit too long.

That skin missing from round my ankles? That's where the Once-born started to eat me. It lives on keratin, you see. That's right—the protein you find in skin and hair and nails and feathers and claws. It's a good job for me my socks are nylon and my shoes have plastic uppers. Otherwise I'd really have been in a mess! Yes, sirree!

Redpath reviewed the account of the past three days which he had been going to present to Leila. It began at breakfast time on Tuesday, with his hindsighted belief that Albert had appeared briefly on his doorstep with the intention of warning him, and had himself been frightened off by a vision of how the Once-born could repay treachery. Albert featured prominently in the mid-part of the story, too—whisking Redpath off to America on the instantaneous magic carpet of psychokinesis and deliberately letting him see what the Once-born did to human beings. And, of course, Albert had played the most important role of all in the final climactic scene. Everything had hinged around the handicapped, doomed, heroic little man—but where was Albert now? Was there any point in telling Leila that Albert and the others had probably been consumed in the huge open-hearth furnace of the Calbridge steelworks, but that it might have been in a volcano or at the centre of the Earth or at the centre of the sun?

How could she believe what he had to say? Looking back on the entire nightmare, how could he believe it himself?

"John, I asked you what you'd done to yourself," Leila said.

He looked at her abstractedly for several seconds, coming to a decision. "I jabbed my shoulder on a spike that was sticking out of a wall, and after that I spilled some acid around my ankles."

"Then I'd better get you to the hospital." She put the car into gear and accelerated away from Raby Street. "Some people shouldn't be allowed out alone."

"I'm one of them. What do you think we could do about it?"

"*That* is the most inelegant proposal I've ever heard of," Leila commented, keeping her gaze on the road ahead. "I suppose I should consider it on those grounds alone."

"Do that," Redpath said, easing himself down in the seat, turning his thoughts away from a past which was growing more unreal with every fleeting second, and towards a future whose realities had yet to emerge from the haze of shifting probabilities.